DOWN A DIRT ROAD

A NOVEL BY

GWEN DELP

Paperback: 979-8-9933998-1-2
Library of Congress Number: 2026908997
Originally published August 2021 with Kindle Direct Publishing.

Cover design by Riley Earle
Layout by Riley Earle
Cover Photography by Tiffany Delp

Printed in the USA in partnership with Village Books.

This book is dedicated to my parents, Ken and Virginia Puyear and my parents-in-law, Boyd and Gertrude Delp.

Family Tree

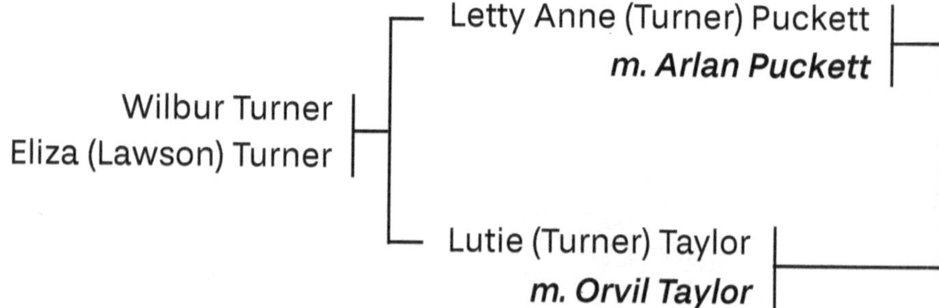

Letty Anne (Turner) Puckett
m. Arlan Puckett
Wilbur Turner
Eliza (Lawson) Turner
Lutie (Turner) Taylor
m. Orvil Taylor

Lulu Puckett
m. Ira Burns
dec. Irene Burns
— Lily
— Rose

Toady Puckett

Rayleen Puckett

Arlan Puckett
m. Maggie (Jones) Puckett
— Wally, Jess, Aaron & Patsy

Biddy (Elizabeth Puckett) Butters
m. Bill Butters
— Burt, Warren & Carl

Birdie (Dorthy Puckett) Caster
m. Willard Caster
— Tootsie, Susie & Casey

Ticky (Pauline) Puckett

Podrick Randall Taylor
m. Carol (Simpson) Taylor
— Jim, John, Joe, Jack & Jerry

Basil (died in WW2)

Darla (Taylor) Jones
div. Jake Wright
m. Bryce Jones
— Rose
— William

Contents

CHAPTER 1

Home

It was Fall and the ground was dry and dusty. Leaves crunched under his feet as he swung his sack of spuds. He was bringing them back from Aunt Lutie's house. He was not supposed to be swinging them, but he was eight years old and that is what he wanted to do. One slipped out and rolled down the hill to his left toward the dried-up creek bed. He slid down the embankment and fetched it. No good to go home with any less than he was sent for. His portion would be the one that suffered he figured.

As he was climbing back up to the road, he heard a horse whinny and he dropped down low to see who it was, just to be careful. He was a Puckett and everyone did not like his kind. He knew if it were the Caster brothers he could expect to be chased, maybe switched or even worse. He had not seen them for a couple of weeks, dodging them whenever he thought they might be around. The last time they caught him they cut a big hunk of hair out of the top of his head and it still did not lay down right on top.

The horse was walking slow, no trotting. The rider was not familiar to him. He was an older man with a straw hat on and the horse was a sorry looking creature that probably could not trot. The rider did not notice Arlan Puckett crouched down in the weeds with his sack of spuds. He was looking straight ahead. He looked like Arlan's Pa, but he had not seen him for a long time, so he was not too sure about that.

Once the rider passed, Arlan crept back up to the road and followed at a safe distance, always looking behind him and keeping an eye on the rider too. After about a mile it was time for Arlan to turn left off the road toward his family's place. The rider turned the same way and next thing Arlan knew, he was hitching his horse to the rail fence in the front part of their yard.

It was not much of a yard. It was simply hard dirt with some chickens pecking around old wheels, from old wagons that had long since stopped working. There was a broken wooden wagon that no one could remember ever using and an old cast iron tub that the little girls had pulled up from the back of the house to play in. It was in front of a house that was unpainted with a slanted porch. The steps up to it were made from flat rocks that someone had hauled up from somewhere and laid down as steps. The door was open and the sound of a sewing machine could be heard coming from the house. It was late afternoon and the sun was behind the hill and the yard and house were in shadow. A small curl of smoke was rising from the chimney.

Arlan waited to see what the stranger was going to do before he went in the house. The stranger dismounted and just stood there for what seemed like an hour. He was just staring at the house and putting in a fresh plug of tobacco. Whoever this was they were not in a hurry to go into the house or to let anyone know they were there.

Before Arlan could go in, the little girls came out, all three of them in their dirty rag dresses and their hair in untidy braids. Biddy was seven, Birdie was six, and Ticky was five. Momma had a child each year until Pa left. There were three older than Arlan, all girls. He was tucked right in the middle of all the girls. There was a gap between Arlan and the older girls of 5 years, so they were thirteen, fourteen, and fifteen.

Biddy did the talking for the three littles and she said, "Who you?"

The rider grinned and said, "I is your Pa, little Biddy."

Biddy stuck out her tongue and said, "No you ain't. We ain't got no Pa. You better git outta here."

Arlan thought, "That is Biddy. She don't take nothing off nobody."

The rider chuckled and said, "Then how's come I know you are Biddy, that's Birdie, that's Ticky and standing behind me is Arlan."

Arlan jumped at that and ran around the rider and up onto the porch with his sisters. He looked hard at the rider who was still just standing by his horse, chewing his fresh plug of tobacco.

Biddy said, "You is too old to be our Pa. He ain't old like youense is. You is just an old goat."

At that the rider slapped his leg and started laughing, which brought on coughing, and spitting and generally distasteful sounds coming out of what sounded like a chest full of rocks. Arlan stepped in front of his little sisters and said, "Ifens you are our Pa, what is our Ma's name?"

"Well, Arlan, her name is Letty Anne. And your older sisters are Lulu, Toady, and Rayleen. So, you see, I knowed all of you!"

Before Arlan could say anything else, Mama

came to the door. She was a little woman with her hair pulled up tight in a bun on the nape of her neck. She was just thirty, but she was already wrinkled from the dry air, the hard work, the worry, the childbearing, and all the other things that made women age quickly in this part of the country. She seldom smiled as she was ashamed of her teeth. The front ones were broken out and the bottom ones were black with decay. She had on a loose house dress that had faded long ago and was tied around her waist by a graying apron made from a flour sack. Her eyes were squinting as she needed glasses and she stared hard at the rider. Then she said, "Hello Abel."

It had been three years since she had seen him and this is all she had to say. He had left one day before the sun came up. The kids asked where he was and she said, "Gone." That was it; no more, no less. That was Letty Anne Puckett, a woman of few words. They had been scraping by since he left, just like it was before he left, so maybe Letty Anne did not mind. She had not had another baby in five years, so maybe that was why she did not care. But that was just speculation on the older girls' part.

Arlan was still looking the rider over and not quite ready to believe that was his Pa. He looked like him all right, but he was only five the last time he saw him. He just was not ready to accept that this man who had slowly rode that broken down horse into their yard was his Pa, Abel Puckett.

When the Caster boys caught him, they would always say things like, "You is as no good as your old man, Abel Puckett. You gonna be a lyin' cheat who don't take no care of yer family, jest like him. You is nothing, Arlan Puckett."

Arlan would always try to scream back, "He is so good. He is comin' back here, youense will see!", but now he was standing here. He was not sure he was not all the bad things they said about him. He was not much to look at and he did not have a pack on the horse even. That means, no food for them, not even a sack of spuds like Arlan was holding. He turned and walked into the house and put the sack on the table that stood in the middle of the big room that was the living area, the kitchen, the bath house, and the bedroom for all of them. He looked back at the open door and thought, "Where is he gonna sleep? Not on my mattress, that's for dang sure."

Arlan threw open the back door and headed toward the woods. He would just stay away for a while and see what happened when he came back. He always took off the first chance he got. He could hide and never be found if he wanted and right now, that sounded like the thing to do. Stay away from the Caster boys and stay away from that man who says he is Abel Puckett. Arlan knew how to survive. He had grabbed a cold biscuit off the counter before he left and that should hold him over if he wanted to stay out there all night. He grabbed his old barn coat that he inherited from his cousin Pod, worn almost through on the elbows, but still with a flannel lining that kept him warm enough. He disappeared through the brush.

When the three older girls came home that day, they were surprised to see the old nag tied at the fence. They had walked home from the jobs they had just recently secured. Lulu was working at the store in Noble, helping Mr. Burns with sweeping and keeping the windows washed and the scales clean. She was getting about 20 hours a week and it was welcome cash for the family.

Toady was working for Mr. Burns' wife, ironing and helping with the little twins she had given birth to six months before. Mrs. Burns (as she insisted Toady call her) was not well before she had the twins and she was doing much worse now, spending a lot of time lying down and crying. Rayleen did not have a job, but Mrs. Burns let Toady bring her along to help out as there was a lot of work to be done.

Lulu started up the steps and was stopped by Biddy, who was out of breath and talking as fast as she could. "If youense go in there you is gonna see an ugly old man says he is our Pa! He too ugly to be our Pa. "

Lulu pushed past Biddy, taking her hand as she walked into the house. It was dusk now and the lamps were lit on the table and in the kitchen. A fire was going in the cook stove and the littlest girls were sitting on the rug playing with their rag dolls and sneaking glances at the man who was seated in Mama's rocker by the fireplace. Mama was standing at the sink, peeling some spuds. Lulu put down her bag and took out a hunk of bacon that Mr. Burns had given her and slipped on her apron to start making biscuits. She looked harder and said, "Hi Pa."

He grinned and showed his tobacco stained teeth and said, "Well howdy Lil' Lulu. You is all growed up now isn't ya?"

Lulu turned her back on him and started mixing the dough for biscuits. Toady and Rayleen went to get water and did not say a word to Abel. Biddy asked "Where's Arlan at Mama?"

Mama just shook her head and said, "I reckon he will come around in a bit. You know how he is when strangers come around."

Pa cleared his throat and said, "Hold on now Letty Anne, I ain't no stranger. You done spoilt that kid ifen he gits to hide out when he pleases. I'll switch his hide when he gits back here."

Mama did not respond, but Lulu knew her Mama and no one was going to switch Arlan. Especially not the man who went off and left them to fend for themselves three years before. Lulu popped the biscuits in the oven and after she washed up, she set the table. Toady and Rayleen came in with the water and asked Mama what else she needed them to do. Mama said, "Wash up and comb your hair. Supper is almost ready." Then she pulled Toady aside and whispered, "Maybe holler for Arlan out back. He is just holed up in one of his hidin' spots."

When supper was ready the Puckett's, minus Arlan, sat down to eat around the old table that Mama had moved into the shack when her mama died. It was long and it ran almost the full length of the front room. The chairs were assorted, some made by Uncle Orvil, Aunt Lutie's husband, some from junk piles the kids found when other families left the area. The dishes were an assortment of tin plates, chipped china and Ticky still ate out of the one baby dish that the family had ever owned. It was a china bowl with a little lamb painted in the bottom. It had belonged to Mama when she was a baby. It had a few hairline cracks and it was no longer snow white like when it was new, but it was precious to all of them.

Mama said a blessing and they dug into the boiled potatoes, biscuits with bacon gravy, onions, and applesauce. There was enough for everyone to have one helping and when Arlan did not return, Birdie begged for his helping. Mama said no, she would just hold it a while longer. Birdie stuck her chin out and big tears ran down her cheek. In a few years, after she married, Birdie would have a butt 'an axe handle wide'. She never could get enough to eat, even when she married a man who provided well for her and she moved up to Kansas City into a fine house. Birdie loved food and she never forgot what being hungry felt like.

This was the beginning of the time that Abel moved home for a long time. Everyone adjusted and he was just as no good and lazy as before he left. No one asked about where he had been and he did not provide any information. He just started sitting on the crooked porch and rocking in the squeaky rocker. Sometimes he walked over to see his brother, Elmer Puckett and his wife Bessie May. He would come home with a pie, some onions or carrots, sometimes a piece of ham or something else for the family. But he did not seem to be looking for work.

The thing was, there really was not much work. If you had a horse and a plow you could take care of a few crops, if the drought did not dry them up. If you had a cow, you could keep her fed and probably get milk for a while, until she dried up and you had to eat her. If you had chickens you had eggs and meat and if you took good care of them, you had enough to sell.

Letty Anne Puckett raised chickens. She had built herself a chicken shed when she first got married. She had taken the $25 her pa gave her and bought baby chicks at the feed store and supplies for a proper coop. She always kept a flock of layers and once their laying days were over, she let them out to forage for themselves and always had one to catch and butcher for supper. She took her eggs to town, or so Noble was called, although it was not more than a general store, a post office, a tavern, a doctor's house, and a few other houses spread around on dirt roads. She sold to Lulu's boss, Mr. Burns at Burn's General and she used that money for coffee, sugar, salt, and flour. Sometimes she could afford a little fabric and everyone got a new dress, always the same fabric for all of them.

The girls all wanted to have different dress-es, but Mr. Burns gave you a better deal if you bought all the same yardage. If you bought the bolt, then it was the cheapest. One year she bought a bolt of green checked fabric. The girls hated it. The fabric faded to gray and it wore out so fast. Mama complained to Mr. Burns, but he just said, "I cain't help you Letty Anne. I just sell what the man give me."

At the time Abel returned they were all wearing a blue flower print with little yellow flowers on it. It was better fabric and some of the dresses still looked pretty. Biddy, Birdie and Ticky's dresses were the worst as they got so dirty playing out in the woods and the dirt all day. But they were less concerned than the older girls. Lulu was making money now and so was Toady and they were planning on new dresses soon. They were lucky to get work, but Mama had raised them to be polite and they had always impressed Mr. Burns with their manners. Mama always insisted, hair combed and clean, fingernails clean when you go to town, speak softly and no swears. The only one Mama had trouble with was Biddy. She was not one to follow anyone's orders. Biddy made up all her own orders and she and Pa got into it nearly every day after he came home.

Biddy would tell him it was "time youense got off that porch and chopped wood". She would stick out her tongue when he was sitting there and then run away taunting him. He complained to Letty Anne about her behavior, but Mama just shook her head and said, "That's your daughter, Abel."

Biddy ran Birdie and Ticky. Whatever she said they should do, they did it. She was the one who nicknamed Ticky, whose real name was Pauline. One day Ticky sat down in the dirt and just started screaming and saying, "The tickies, they is all over me! Mama, the tickies is eatin' me!" Biddy ran and got Mama and she started with the hot match heads and pliers, pulling the ticks off of poor little Pauline. Her whole bottom was covered. She had been sitting on a pile of leaves in the woods watching Birdie fish in the little trickle of a creek and the "tickies" had attacked her. From that day on she was always known as Ticky.

Biddy also named Birdie, whose real name was Dorothy. Dorothy loved birds when she was a little toddler and she would run off chasing them when Biddy was trying to keep her close by for Mama. That is why she was known as Birdie, because she loved birds.

Biddy herself was named Elizabeth and Biddy was an accepted nickname for Elizabeth in her family, so she had never been called anything but Biddy. She liked her name and when Arlan teased her and said, "You is just like old Mabel down at the river. Ever one says she is an old biddy!" Biddy flipped her braids and paid him no mind. She liked her name 'just fine' and she called herself that her whole life. It just felt right and she knew she was always right and that was the way it always was for Biddy. She married a man who believed it too and when she told him he had to go to work for the post office, he took the civil service exam and passed it, just like she said he would. When he went off to World War II, she said, "You get your ass home Bill Butters, in one piece and that includes your brain" and he did. Biddy was a force on the planet and no one ever wanted to get in her way. Even when Arlan teased her when she got married for being Biddy Butters, she did not pay him any attention. Even old Abel learned to leave her alone. There was a time when she fixed him good.

One afternoon she hatched a plan to fool Abel into thinking they found some money. It was not because Abel spent a lot of money. He bought tobacco, but he did not drink and he never purchased the home supplies. But if he had some money, he always kept it. Once in a while he might come home with a pair of new overalls or a pocketknife and that made Mama so mad. So Biddy got the idea that she would claim to have seen some money down the old outhouse hole that Uncle Orvil had dug for them last year. Right now they were without an outhouse and had just been going up behind the collapsed old barn, but last year they had planned to have an outhouse and Uncle Orvil dug it, but no one ever got around to putting a structure over it. So once it was half filled with their sewage, everyone just started using the rest of the woods.

Biddy came tearing around the house that morning, faking excitement and hollering, "Pa, there is money in the outhouse hole! I seed it!

Looks like someone lost it out of their pocket when they was poopin'. Looks like a whole damn roll of it! You gotta come and get it. I cain't reach it no how. Hurry up Pa!"

Abel jumped out of the chair so fast. No one had ever seen him move like that. In fact most people had bad nicknames for him and Uncle Orvil always said, "That man is cut dog lazy." (Translation: when you neuter a male dog, they usually become less energetic.) So Abel hot foots it to the outhouse hole and bends over, looking for the money. He said, "Biddy, I cain't see no money in there."

Biddy shouts, "Them leaves blew on top of it. I cain't reach it. You gotta get down on your knees to fetch it." Abel squatted down and peered into the outhouse hole. Just then Biddy screamed as loud as she could, scared Abel and he went headfirst down into the hole! It was a scene to behold.

Biddy was rolling on the grass laughing and her little sisters were imitating her. Abel was shouting and scrambling and was stuck in the hole. He was shouting for Mama. When she made it to the back yard, she found Abel knee deep in old sewage, leaves and offal stuck in his hair, trying to pull himself up out of the hole. Mama stopped short and shouted, "You fool Abel. What are you doin' in that outhouse hole? You crazy? What are you doin' in there?"

Abel stopped shouting and his voice went deep and hard. "When I git out of this here hole, I am gonna switch that Biddy till she cain't walk no more."

Mama said, "You will do no such thing." She handed him a hoe handle and he pulled himself out of the muck. Then she said, "Go to the creek and try to wash some of that off. I ain't lettin' you back in the house with that crap all over ya." She stomped back in the house and Abel was too ashamed to tell her why he was in the hole.

Biddy, Birdie, and Ticky were long gone when he got himself cleaned up and they did not show up until supper time. Not another word was said about the incident, but the little girls always liked to tell the story of "our stupid Pa diving for dollars in the shit hole!"

Eventually Arlan came back to the house. He stayed gone about ten days, going over to Aunt Lutie's for food and hanging out with his cousins Pod, Basil and Darla. He was always welcome at Aunt Lutie's. She and Uncle Orvil had more money and more food than at his house and they only had three kids. Pod was sixteen and he worked full time for a farmer one county over. He rode his horse over on Sunday night and stayed until Saturday afternoon at the farmer's house in the barn. Then he rode back home and helped Uncle Orvil with whatever needed to be done at home. Pod was considered an excellent worker and everyone was so proud of him. He always treated his Mama and his younger brother and sister well and he always worked and gave his family most of the money. Arlan thought he was the best person he knew and he wished Pod could be his pa.

Arlan never did take to his Pa. He always felt that he was an embarrassment. The teasing he got, the comments he heard, but most of all the way Abel Puckett lived his life, did not make for a great father figure for anyone. So Arlan always looked elsewhere for guidance. Uncle Orvil was kind and Pod was a great role model, but the real guidance in Arlan's life came from his Aunt Lutie.

Lutie was Letty Anne's sister. They had grown up together, even though they were really half-sisters. Their parents got married when Letty Anne was just a little baby and Lutie was a toddler. Lutie's father, Wilbur, was widowed after Lutie was born when her mother died in childbirth. He looked hard for someone to take care of his little daughter and when he found Eliza, he thought he had found the best, which he had. She got pregnant before they could get married, but that did not matter. She moved in and took on the care of Lutie and their new little Letty Anne. Wilbur was terrified of losing another wife to childbirth and he and Eliza agreed they would try hard not to have any more babies and they did it.

So Lutie and Letty Anne had grown up in a small family, especially for those times when women did not have many options for not having babies. Their mother was a good person and she took such good care of the girls. They did not have a lot of money, but they were taught to be clean, polite, and most of all to be able to be accomplished at all the things girls needed to know how to do to keep a house and home. They had chickens and pigs to care for and were expected to earn money as soon as they hit twelve years old. They were taught to stick up for each other and always do their school lessons. They got the best that Eliza and Wilbur had to give. So when Lutie took Arlan under her wing, he had another person he could mold his life from.

Letty Anne did not resent Arlan's time with her sister and family. She had made a bad choice in Abel when she was still a child and she felt it was her cross to bear. She had a good handle on the girls. They looked to her for guidance and they felt their father was just a burden their mother felt she had to bear. In all truth, the only one who liked him even a little was Birdie. She was shy and she always followed Biddy, but she thought her Pa was sweet and she would sneak up on his lap or bring him coffee or fetch him a good whittling stick when he asked.

Letty Anne could never forget how she ended up with Arlan Puckett. She was just fourteen, going on fifteen. Her family always went to Sunday service at the little church just outside of Noble. It was called the Rocky Point Baptist Church because it had been built on a pile of rocks. It was a simple little building, but the rock foundation was pretty and the ladies of the church kept the flower beds planted and groomed. In the summer, every Sunday, some-one brought a fresh bouquet from their yard. In the Fall it was decorated with colored leaves and elder berry branches and in the winter, pine branches with cones graced the altar.

Letty Anne and Lutie sang in the small choir and Pastor John T. Porter was the choir direc-tor. He had a strong baritone and he led the choir with his guitar, which he played beau-tifully. Every Wednesday at 4:00 they walked to the church for choir practice. There were ten people allowed in the choir, five males and five females. The Puckett sisters tried out for their spots at thirteen and they were accept-ed as they had lovely soprano voices. Several older ladies complained because their girls did not make the cut, but Pastor Porter was not bothered by it and said very firmly, "The best singers are up front and all the other singers need to spread throughout the church. They help keep the melody strong. You ladies ought to be more concerned with the whole church and not your daughter's performance." Most of the women were quieter about it, but there was still gossiping. They called Lutie and Letty Anne Turner, Pastor Porter's Prissies and some other less kind terms. Eliza told her daughters, keep singing, even better, and do what the Pastor tells you to do.

So one Wednesday, Letty Anne walked the two miles to church alone. She was singing as she walked and the sound was reverberating through the woods. She was a picture, walking and singing. Her hair was long and brown and it was braided down her back with a blue ging-ham ribbon tied on the end. She was shape-ly and she had on a blue and white gingham dress that matched her blue eyes perfectly. She did not realize how pretty she was just yet and she was happy to be out in the beautiful spring weather, hands out of the garden dirt.

Abel was riding his horse down the same dirt road when he saw her. He knew who she was, but he lived in the next county and he had never spoken to her. He had watched her grow-ing up when he would ride by her Pa's house and see her hoeing in the garden or hanging out wash. She was a cute little thing since he could remember and seeing her today in the speckled shade, singing with a voice like a bird, he just stopped and stared. Letty Anne noticed him and stopped up short. He said, "Hello Miss Turner."

Letty Anne politely said, "Hello. I am afraid I cain't 'member yer name."

He stepped off his horse and said, "Arlan Puckett, m'am. I live over yonder in the next county. Pleased to meet ya."

Letty Anne said, "Hello Mr. Puckett. I is walkin' to choir practice and I gotta get goin' or I might be late. Pastor Porter likes us to get there on time." She continued walking and passed Arlan close enough for him to smell her freshly washed hair and to notice the way her hips filled out her dress. He was eighteen now and he was ready for marriage and Miss Letty Anne Turner was looking like a good prospect.

Although Abel turned out to be good for nothing, he was working at eighteen and he had his own horse for riding, a horse and plow for loan, and a couple of cows along with a bull. He had built himself a small shack close to his parents and still ate his meals at their house. He had a big family. There were ten kids and their mother had been dead since the last one was born. His older sisters Fran and Nan kept the house and took care of the small ones. Abel helped some but he was focused on getting a wife and starting a family. He did not want to hang around with his siblings and his bossy sisters any more than he had too.

Letty Anne thought he was handsome and she mentioned that to Lutie. Lutie cautioned her and said, "The Pucketts are a wild bunch. You best think hard afore you go lookin' at one of them!"

Letty Anne had heard stories too. The boys were known for drinking and running wild and the sisters were known for being fighters. In fact there was a story about Fran and Nan beating up their oldest brother's wife when she claimed they were making biscuits the wrong way. One grabbed her hair and the other one pushed her face in the plate of biscuits and gravy she was eating. The wife left and did not return and her husband had to go all the way to Springfield to get her back. She took a train to her Aunt's house and said she was done with the Pucketts. But she came back with her husband and she stayed away from Fran and Nan.

But Abel was determined and he found every chance he could to see Letty Anne. He came to church every Sunday, even though he had never come before. He stood and sang loudly and off key and he waited outside to greet the Turner Family each time church was over. This prompted Wilbur and Eliza to ask Letty Anne if she had taken an interest in Abel Puckett. She blushed and said, "Yes. I like him."

Eventually Eliza asked him after Sunday service if he would like to come over and eat Sunday dinner with them. Abel said, "Yes m'am. Thank ya. What time do youense eat?"

Eliza told him to come in a half hour and there he was, hair combed, clean shirt, clean overalls and his dress up shoes. Wilbur invited him to sit on the opposite side of the table as Letty Anne and Abel bowed his head while Wilbur said grace.

After that he came to most Sunday dinners and when he felt he was accepted, he asked if he and Letty Anne could take a horseback ride down to the pond, which was not far away. Wilbur agreed and said be back in an hour. Abel helped Letty Anne up on the horse and he walked beside her, leading his horse and talking up a blue streak. He told Letty Anne about all of his plans for the future. He wanted a big house with a front porch and a nice barn and a chicken shed and of course a solid outhouse. He talked about his wife wearing dresses she made on the sewing machine he would buy her and the babies he hoped would come. He painted a good picture and Letty Anne could see it all too and it was just what she wanted. She finally giggled during one of their walks and said, "Ain't youense gonna ask me to marry ya, Abel?"

Abel let out a whoop and dropped down to

the ground in front of the horse and said, "Letty Anne Turner, will you marry me?"

Letty Anne grabbed the reins from him and hit the horse's flank and took off at gallop laughing. She circled back around and jumped off the horse and Abel caught her in his arms. He said, "Let's go ask your Pa."

That was the beginning and things were good for the newlyweds for a year or two. The older girls were born in the first two years and Letty Anne did not have any trouble with child-birth, though her father fretted that he would lose a daughter like he lost his wife. But Letty Anne had seven children all together and each one was healthy and so was she.

Lulu was born first and shortly thereafter came Toady (called Toady because she had a birth mark that looked like a toad on her right thigh) and then came Rayleen. By the time Rayleen came along, Abel had started to act differently than he had when he and Letty Anne first married. He started playing cards with a group of fellows who met over at Bachelor Tom's place. Then the bull got sick and died and then the cows dried up and then it was just a long string of small disappointments. Letty Anne kept her head on her shoulders and just kept working hard to keep it all together, but Abel seemed to be slipping into the kind of role his father had always filled. Lazy, no good, big smile, sleeping on the porch, let the women do the chores kind of man. It had run Abel's mother into an early grave and Lutie reminded her little sister of what happened to Ma Puckett. But Letty Anne still loved Abel at that point and she thought she might be able to help him turn it around.

Meanwhile, no more babies were made as she told Abel that was not going to happen unless he found a way to take better care of them. That was the first time Abel took off. He stayed gone for four years that time. Rumor was he would go to Kansas City and find work or beg on the streets or shack up with some no good woman, but no one ever really knew for sure what he did, except Abel himself.

When Abel returned, he handed over $100 in cash to Letty Anne. He told her he would keep making money if she would please, just let him come home to her and her bed. Letty Anne still loved Abel. She still had a little thrill in the pit of her stomach when she saw him. She still loved his kisses and besides, the girls could use a father, especially if he could just work for a while.

He did work for a while. He talked to his brother Elmer and Elmer's father-in-law hired him on at his sawmill. Abel worked steady for a couple years. It was a fairly good time for the Pucketts. Arlan was born and then Biddy and Letty Anne was pregnant with Birdie when things got tight again. The sawmill ran out of work and Abel came home one day and he was drunk. Abel was not a drinking man. He could not hold his liquor and it made him desperately sick. He laid in the yard, where Letty Anne told the children he had to stay and moaned and groaned and finally hollered, "Letty Anne, I is sorry, but I ain't got no work. I drank that moon shine Letty Anne, youense gotta help me get over this here sickness so I can go look for work. Please Letty Anne..."

Letty Anne just did her work and let him lie. Toady felt sorry for him and she tried to help him by bringing him some water, but he puked that up too. Lulu got a willow switch and hit him over and over on the butt and called him a "no good lazy ass poor excuse for a man". Letty Anne asked her to stop swearing but as soon as she was out of ear shot, she started in on him again.

The story goes that Abel did not work again. No one was so sure how Ticky was conceived, but somehow that seventh child came along and when she was born, he only stayed for about two years before he disappeared again. This time Letty Anne decided it was time to just get on with life like he was never going to be in it again.

CHAPTER 2

Every Day

Arlan had an idea about what he wanted to do, but it did not mean staying in Missouri where he was born and raised. He wanted to go out west and grow apples and peaches and see real mountains. He had looked at a magazine at Aunt Lutie's house that had pictures of the Pacific Northwest and he loved the scenes of what was called the Yakima Valley the most. There was a picture of an orchard sloping out and away and, in the distance, a huge mountain on the horizon. The trees had pink and white blossoms and the caption read: Apples blooming with Mount Adams in the distance. He asked if he could cut out the picture and he folded it up carefully and carried it in his pocket. Whenever he had some time, he would take it out and gaze at the blossoming trees and the snowcapped mountain in the distance. That is where he wanted to be and he was sure he would get there.

Arlan did not share this with anyone for a long time. Besides, everyone was so busy trying to get by in a dry and hard scrabble place. Dreaming of mountains and orchards was not something they had time for. He spent more time at home once he got used to the idea of Abel living there. He did not like his father, nor did he really give him much attention, but he loved his mama and he helped her as much as he could. He knew that once he could find a way to earn money, he would help her for a time before he ever left. For now all he could do was help her with the chickens.

Arlan was not crazy about the chickens. In fact, he hated them. For one thing, they smelled awful and when it was hot out and he had to help clean the coop he would tie two kerchiefs over his nose and mouth and periodically go around the back of the house and puke. It was not because Letty Anne was a bad chicken farmer, it was just that she kept so many and when they came into roost at night, Arlan was sure all they did was poop while they slept. Cleaning up the laying boxes was easier and he would scrub her waterers and feeders for her every few weeks. But mucking out the pure chicken shit was gruesome. He would put it in a wheelbarrow and then take it to the big pile they kept below the dilapidated barn. They had not had a cow for a long time and Abel came home with his one broken down horse and it had already died off. The barn was starting to lean and Arlan was sure it was just going to go ahead and fall.

Arlan did not go to school around the time his father returned. In fact, he had only gone for a couple of years. The teacher they were used to being taught by, died of influenza and the substitute was a kid who had only gone through eighth grade. He could not keep the classroom under control, so Arlan just stopped going, right along with the rest of the Puckett kids. The older girls had helped the little ones learn to read and Arlan could read, write and do enough math to get by. School was not anything to strive for in their part of the world. School did not bring you anymore good fortune, unless you were brave enough or fool hardy enough to go to a city and work. Everyone who stayed told themselves and each other that it was useless as "the world is only as big as where ya come from".

If you wanted to say who Arlan felt the closest to in his family, that would be his big sister Lulu. She thought differently than the rest.

She was quiet most of the time and when she did speak up everyone tended to listen to her. He knew he did and when he finally got the courage to show her the picture of the western orchards and mountain, she sat down on the stump where she was chopping kindling and looked it over carefully. She said, "Arlan, that is a beautiful place. I agree that you need to go there. You can do it." Then she handed him the picture and said, "Just keep it between us Arlan. Mama don't need to worry and anyone else will try to tell you that you cain't do it." She picked up the ax and went back to chopping. That was what he liked about Lulu. She did not feel the need to boss him around or lecture him or even ask him what he was thinking. She just went one step in front of the other and stayed pretty calm, except when it came to their father and then she could get pretty angry.

Arlan was unaware that Lulu herself had been thinking hard about how to escape this piece of scrappy dirt and broken down adults. First, she had work at Burn's General and that was good. Mr. Burns trusted her with a lot. He even started letting her run the register if he needed to run home to do something for Mrs. Burns or if he wanted to do some bookkeeping in the back or talk to a salesman over a shot of whiskey in his office. Lulu had learned a lot about the business and she even had begun to offer some suggestions that Mr. Burns said he would take under consideration.

One of these ideas was running a sale on fabric, 5 yards at 25% off the regular price for one week. Then back to the regular price the next week. She told him if he bought a higher quality fabric, lowered the price temporarily so women could try it and then once they realized it was much better, raise the price back to the original. He decided it was worth a shot and he even let her pick the fabrics from the salesman who came by monthly with swatches.

As Lulu touched the fabrics she thought of her own mama and the way she slaved away at making dresses and shirts and always just pieced together scraps for her own dresses. So she picked fabrics that would complement each other; such as blue stripes that would look good with a small blue floral print or yellow polka dot to mix with orange and yellow prints. She went for the higher fiber count. When Mr. Burns saw the bill he balked, but she carefully explained how they would still make a profit if they tried out her method. Lulu knew nothing about supply and demand or anything else related to business, but she was smart and Mr. Burns had come to trust her instincts.

The first time Lulu saw her mama in a dress made from two coordinating fabrics she smiled and did not say a word. It worked. Her little sisters were in dresses made from two different fabrics instead of all the same and her mama had taken the leftovers and made herself a very handsome dress with yellow polka dot pockets and collar.

Mr. Burns relied on Lulu more and more. One day as they were taking inventory after the store closed, he asked her for something she could not do for him. Lulu was on her hands and knees pulling some boxes from the back of a low shelf when she felt Mr. Burns hand on her behind. At first, he just laid it gently on her hip, but then he started to massage her. She jumped up and turned to face him and saw his shame and hu-miliation. His face was red and his crotch had a bulge and he whispered, "I am so sorry Lulu." But he still had her pinned in a narrow row of shelves and he did not step away.

Lulu was finding it hard to get her breath and calm down, but she managed to say, "I ain't gonna do nothin' like that Mr. Burns. Youense a married man."

Mr. Burns looked at her and said, "Yes I am. But you know what Mrs. Burns is like Lulu..."

Well yes, Lulu knew all about Mrs. Burns. Her sisters Toady and Rayleen kept her informed every night as they settled into sleep, all three of them on a double bed mattress. Rayleen talked the most. She could not believe all the things she saw in that house. Her biggest amazement was the amount of time Mrs. Burns stayed in bed. "She just lays there until noon or longer. She don't move. Her eyes is open and the babies are cryin', but she don't move. Me and Toady just done took over that house, Lulu. We do everythin', and I mean we even have to wipe her butt sometimes!"

Toady said, "She is a really sick lady. I mean, she cain't even sweep right. I tried to help her to learn some things but it is useless. She ain't able to even shake out a rug. She is so sick."

Rayleen scoffed, "She ain't sick, she just plain lazy! She ain't never been able to do shit. You knows that."

Toady seemed to have a stronger attachment to Mrs. Burns, whom she occasionally referred to as Irene. For some reason she felt sympathetic toward her and she did the personal care for Mrs. Burns when she would let her, like brush out her long blonde hair and braid it and give her a bath with some of her nice, scented soaps from the General Store. But she knew that Mrs. Burns was "teched" in the head. She knew she was not going to get any better and she was determined she was going to keep taking care of the twin baby girls, Rose and Lily.

All this and more had been told to Lulu, but her idea of a future was not screwing Ira Burns in the back of the store, getting pregnant and being made to raise another one of his kids right under his nose. She thought the Burns were getting enough from the Puckett sisters.

She finally pushed Mr. Burns aside and said quietly and politely, "Please do not do that again and I can keep helpin' youense here at the store." Mr. Burns shook his head yes and it never happened again, but it did not mean that Ira Burns did not fall more in love with Lulu as time went on.

What Lulu wanted in life was not to be mama. She was not completely sure how that would be possible as opportunities were not lined up in a neat row for a girl in her part of the world or from her kind of family. Basically women got married in their early to mid-teens, had babies, worked their fingers literally to the bone, died young, and put up with whatever their husband brought to the marriage; love, fists, work, no work, drinking, womanizing, whatever he wanted to do. She just saw girls with no choices. But deep inside of Lulu something was alive and aware that she did not have to accept this and it would be hard and take some real courage, but she felt she could pull it off. But what was it?

She did not have a role model or a woman to talk to about it. Once she had talked to Mama when she felt she might have a crush on Rory Caster, one of her brother's tormentors. He was handsome with black hair that was wavy and hung just over his ears. He was tall and lean and he had a way of holding his head, cocked to one side, when he watched her go by him. She asked while they were canning green beans one hot August afternoon as they put in the final batch of jars to be boiled on the wood stove. "Mama, how did you feel when you knew you wanted to marry Pa?"

Her mother never missed a beat. She lowered the jars down into the boiling water, put on the lid and opened the stove lid to poke the fire to make it hotter. She poured a drink of water and then she sat down and said tiredly, "The feelin' ya git for a man don't stay with ya. Once you push out that first little one you is done with lovin' him. Anyway, don't go thinkin' cuz Rory Caster is stealing looks at ya that he is gonna be anthin' less than a scoundrel."

Lulu did not say anything back. But she did not forget what her mother said. From then on, every boy she saw that was cute or charming or friendly, she just repeated to herself, "the feelin' ya git for a man don't stay with ya". That was enough for her.

CHAPTER 3

Irene's Crazy

Irene Burns had always been taken care of. She could not remember a time when she was not pampered and coddled, even after she married Ira Burns. She was raised in Georgia and she was the youngest of a family with five girls. Her father had money, banking money, and her family had come from the slave owning plantations of the rural south. When she was born her father had already made a fortune and their home was large and beautifully modern. Her mother had hired help, some who had been with the family before the civil war. Irene's nanny, Darby, had been the nanny to all five of the girls and when baby Irene came along, she was old, tired, and lenient.

Irene had sweets for breakfast, lost her shoes in the garden, broke her doll's arms, threw fits at the dinner table, and generally behaved like a spoiled little brat.

Her mother was tired too. She was forty when she gave birth to Irene and everyone was sure she would die or have a baby who was compromised. Once Irene came out in perfect form, her mother sighed a great sigh of relief and resigned herself to not parent another little girl. The four older girls had worn her out with dresses and gowns and parties and hair and schooling, etc. She just could not face that all again, at least not with the same intensity. So she looked at Darby and said, "Please take care of this child and give her whatever she wants. I just am too tired, Darby."

Darby adored little Irene. She had huge blue eyes and soft curly blonde hair, big dimples in her cheeks and a tiny little frame. She was full of giggles and mischief, but even at three years old she had a penchant for being languid. She liked to lay on her bed and stare at her ceiling or go into the garden and lay on the chaise lounge and watch the trees sway. Sometimes Darby just stood and watched her, remembering the other four girls running and playing every day until they wiggled out of the bathtub into clean pajamas and fell asleep instantly when their little heads hit the pillow.

But not little Irene. She was different and as she grew, she just became a bigger burden to her parents, who had lost interest in child rearing and were traveling to Europe often.

Darby was always there until she was not. She died when Irene was twelve. It was sudden, no warning. She was in the kitchen talking to Cook (as she had always been referred to) and she just slid off her chair onto the floor. The doctor said it was a massive heart attack at 70 years old. She had lived with Irene's family most of her life. She did not have children of her own and Cook was her distant cousin. When she was buried, the black neighborhood in their town came out in force, but Irene's family did not attend her service. They sent a spread of cheese sandwiches, fried chicken, and lemonade to the church, but not one of them came to say goodbye.

At that time Irene had her first "bed" episode. It was the day after Darby was buried. She would not rise from her bed. Her mother begged her to get up and go to school. Cook brought her french toast with strawberry jam. Her father promised her a new dress, her sisters, some of them were still at home, tried to pull her out of the bed to dress her but she went limp as a rag doll.

After three days they called in a doctor. He told her family she was suffering from grief and to just give her a few more days and she would be up and going back to school. It took six months before that happened. Her mother hired a new "helper" for Irene as she was too old for a nanny. Her name was Olive and she was only sixteen and she too was very lazy. She would sit in Miss Irene's room for hours thumbing through books, looking out the window, playing solitaire, in other words not doing anything that was useful. Cook tried to tell Irene's mother that this girl Olive was useless, but it did not really matter to Irene's mother. She just hired her to keep an eye on Irene and be sure she did not harm herself or do something they could not fix. She felt so removed from her last child. It was as if she did not have a bond with her. She had let Darby do that. This behavior of Irene's was all Darby's fault, according to Irene's mother, so she just did not worry about it.

Eventually Irene decided to resume life and she had to get a tutor so she could enter into eighth grade with her classmates. The tutor became permanent and Irene did not attend school. She became even stranger as she went through puberty. She refused to go anywhere and spent her days in the house, with the tutor, who was also helping Olive learn to read and write. Irene was devoted to Olive and vice versa. They could spend hours doing nothing together. Irene's mother and father had re-signed themselves to the strangeness of their daughter. They just let her continue with her odd behaviors without intervention.

When Irene was nearing eighteen, her parents left for England for a two month visit with relatives. The older girls were married and scattered and the only people left at home were Irene, Cook, Olive and the gardener. Her parents were gone for six months, not two, and the household took on its own rhythm when they were gone.

First, they did not eat in the dining room anymore. The kitchen became the hub of activity. Breakfast was sweet rolls ordered from the bakery, lunch was peanut butter and jelly sandwiches, supper was chocolate cake and milk or anything else Miss Irene wanted. Cook felt so sorry for little Irene, always left behind, weird little person. She had even gained affection for Olive, simpleton that she was. The three of them and the gardener spent many evenings sitting at the kitchen table playing cards and talking. They all knew things would be different when "the folks" returned.

Mainly Cook knew that they were going to try and get someone to marry Miss Irene. She had heard them talking about it before they left and it stuck in Cook's mind how callously they spoke of their youngest. They had made some connections with a man in Missouri who had advertised for a bride. He lived in a small town, ran a general store, and had come from decent folks, or so their connections told them. It was arranged that before Irene's nineteenth birthday, he would be brought out to meet her, they would have a small civil ceremony and he would take her away. Away from them, away from all she knew, just away.

When her parents returned from their long trip abroad, they let Irene know that she was going to need to get married and leave home. It was not like this had never been talked about before. It had always been part of conversations since she had turned fifteen, but the time to talk was over. Irene's mother showed her the wardrobe they had purchased for her to wear when she left home and explained to her that she must have the courage to go and live her life. Irene listened and retired to her bed for several weeks. She refused food this time and even her precious Olive could not get her to bathe or dress. One day she showed up at the breakfast table with her hair in tangles and a dressing gown and when her mother started to speak, Irene said, "I will marry someone. I do not care. But I must have Olive."

Her parents were joyous and Mr. Burns was sent for immediately. When he came to Georgia, he met a beautiful girl with blonde curly hair, huge blue eyes, and sweet dimples. She was quiet and polite and accepted his small gifts of ribbons and a velvet pocketbook and a gold pin with pearls for her coat. She thought he was not very handsome to look at, but in her own mind Irene already knew what no one else did. She would never be any different than she was on that day. She would always be sweet, she would always be lazy, she would need time in bed to rest as she was so easily tired, and she would never go without someone to help her get through it all. She had known this since Darby died. She would never move forward from that time, that age, that level of activity. She was stuck there and she would remain there and no one could move her. Period.

So, by the time Ira Burns realized all of this, it was too late and he could not "return" her like a box of damaged goods at the general store. Olive did come with her, but Olive "ran off" once she saw that she was going to be the cook, the maid, the gardener, and the caretaker of Miss Irene. She slipped out the first week and took her wages and hopped on a bus back to Georgia, back to her folks, back to find her own way. Irene did not take this news well and ended up spending a month in bed. Ira was crushed, but he had been a bachelor and he knew how to take care of himself, so he cooked, washed his clothes, ironed and tried to keep things clean.

He told people his new wife was feeling poorly and he just did the best he could, not knowing if it had been worth the money her parents had given him to take her. At the time he did not know why they were willing to give him that much, but he was enamored by her looks and her manners and after all, they sent a freight car full of furniture and house goods before he even put the ring on her finger.

But now that he had her, he realized he had married someone who was "crazy". Oddly, one thing she did not refuse was having sex with him. She was willing to perform her duties and she was very matter of fact about him "doing his business" and she then rolled over and would fall asleep instantly. It was not the romantic idea he had of marriage, but if she did not mind, he could live with it. But when she got pregnant, he had to face the fact that he would have to get help and he would have to keep help, probably for their entire married life. That is when he approached Letty Anne and asked her if one of her girls would like to help him and his wife out with house chores and eventually with childcare. Conversations were had and it ended up that Toady was chosen to take care of Mrs. Burns. When she asked if Rayleen could help her, her mama said that was fine, as long as they both knew they had chores to do at home too.

Irene took to Toady just like she did Darby and Olive. She treated her like her little pet, her little puppy or kitty, but she also expected her to treat her like a little princess. Toady was the perfect match for this as she was full of love and lightness. Ira and Irene Burns were lucky the day they met the Puckett girls. Very lucky...

CHAPTER 4

Spunk

Arlan was about ten when he had a real run in with his father, Abel. It all started when Uncle Orvil gave Arlan a horse of his own. It was an older horse, but not completely worn out. This mare's foaling days had passed and she had been the "pet" he had kept for his younger children to ride. Now they were no longer interested, he thought Arlan might enjoy her. The horse's name was Spunk. She was a pinto mare and she had a thick black mane. Arlan loved that horse. He kept her at Uncle Orvil's for a few weeks and then decided he wanted to take her home so he could ride her back and forth and take his little sisters on rides.

Arlan fixed up a spot in the dilapidated barn

and made a deal with his Uncle Orvil for hay if he hauled it home himself. Lulu bought him some grain at the General Store and things were going along nicely. One morning Arlan went out to feed Spunk to find her gone. The gate to her stall was open, her old bridle was gone. Arlan whistled for her and ran outside hollering her name. He felt like he was going to start crying, but he was too damn mad. Who in the hell would take his horse or worse yet, just let her go? Of course, he knew Spunk and she would not go far, so he ran back in the house to tell his mama he was going looking for the horse. That was when he noticed Abel was not sitting in his usual morning spot by the fire. In fact, his old boots were gone too. Arlan looked at his mama and she said, "I ain't seen him since I got up, so that ain't a good thing Arlan."

Arlan learned about his own temper that day. He started the hunt for his pa on foot. He went to one of the only places his pa went and that was to Uncle Elmer's, his brother. It was a few miles away, so by the time Arlan got there he was good and mad. He had been cussing and kicking dirt clods and throwing rocks at crows all the way there. He had thrown punches in the air and declared he would "kick that old bastard's butt" when he saw him. Arlan was only ten years old, but he was strong and he thought as lazy as his pa was, he could at least knock him over and try to jump him. When he got to Uncle Elmer's he saw Spunk tied to the front porch rail. Spunk whinnied when she saw Arlan and Arlan first untied her and took her to Uncle's barn and threw her a leaf of hay.

Then he headed back to the house to deal with Abel. When he came back Abel was standing on the porch in his overalls, talking to his brother just like he was a regular man; a man who works and takes care of his family and does not live off them, never lifting a finger to help. Abel had a plan and he stood in the yard and said, "Hows come you took Spunk?"

Abel guffawed and said, "Cuzzin' she's our horse."

Arlan lowered his head and said, "I figured you would say that." And before Abel knew what hit him, Arlan had run straight into his pa's legs and knocked him on his butt. Before he could even put his hands down to sit up, Arlan was on top of him, fists flying and cussing up a storm. He called him lazy, no good, son of a bitch, shit head, and coon dog. He hit him in the head and punched him in the gut and Abel finally got a hold of Arlan's fists and forced him over on his back. When he stood up, he went to kick Arlan and was hollering that he had no business thinking that horse was his, but before the blow could land, Uncle Elmer pushed Abel down the porch steps and reached down and pulled Arlan up on his feet.

Uncle Elmer said, "Best get on that there horse and ride on out of here son. Ain't no good gonna come from you and your pa beatin' on each other."

Arlan opened his mouth to protest, but when he looked at the pathetic creature pulling himself off the ground in the yard, he lost all of his fight. That hunk of useless man might have put the seed in his mama, but that man was not his father. His dusty overalls and lank hair falling over his eye, his small pot belly and his pathetically skinny arms were sickening. He jumped off the porch, ran to the barn, hopped on Spunk and galloped out of the yard, not looking back. A switch had flipped in his head and it never did switch back.

When he got home, he asked his mama if he could fix himself up a room out in the barn. She nodded yes and said, "Use whatever younse need honey. You still eat my food though, right?" Arlan nodded and that is when his new "barn room" was built.

Arlan gathered up boards, nails, the hammer, and the old saw. He started out by just drawing in the dirt with a stick, figuring the shape of room he wanted. He wanted an L shape, with Spunk's stall on one side of it. Then he decided he would have a table and a chair in the smaller part of the L and build a small bunk on the wall alongside Spunk. He worked for about five days straight, hammering and sawing. His little sisters took an interest and started hanging out in the barn watching him. Biddy gave advice about how he needed to fix the roof so no rain would get in. Rayleen and Toady hauled his old mattress out and gave it a good beating with the broom before they took it into his bunk. Lulu brought him a flannel blanket she made from discounted fabric at the General Store. Mama found an old wash basin and towel for him. Spunk loved all the activity and never kicked at the little ones as they climbed over the stall wall and under her hooves.

One morning Abel came out to the barn room. Arlan turned his back when he saw him and Abel said, "I kin take that horse ifen I want boy."

Abel turned and narrowed his eyes at his pa and said, "I will kill ya. You best keep one eye open old man." Abel never came back to visit the barn room again.

CHAPTER 5

The Dolls

Toady had a secret and she wanted to tell someone. She wanted to tell Rayleen, but she knew her sister was going to pick it all apart and take away the joy she felt in her secret. She wanted to tell Lulu, but Lulu would "drag her ass out of that old coot's house" the minute she told her. So she stewed on it for a while and told no one. Her sisters knew something was going on and they teased her and taunted her trying to get her to say what was on her mind, but she just tucked her head down and could not help but grin.

Toady figured she was in love. She was really pretty certain that was what was going on with her. She was sixteen years old and plenty old enough to get married, let alone fall in love. She was turning out to be a pretty girl, maybe the prettiest one of Letty Anne's. She had long hair that was straight as a stick but was a rich auburn color. She wore it in braids and then wrapped the braids around her head. She had a nice figure and as her mama always said, "You could put that Toady in an old potato sack and she'd still look like a dolly."

Toady had a way with anything she put on. She could take the regular pattern her mama made for a dress; waisted, small gathering in the skirt, just below the knee, pockets in the skirt, and she could fill it out nicely. She always made sure she was clean and while Rayleen would forget to wash her legs and feet after a dusty walk home, Toady always took the time to clean herself up. She learned how to take care of her fingernails by clipping and filing and one day Lulu brought her polish home from the General Store. It was pink and she painted her nails carefully and Rayleen's and the little girls too. Rayleen picked hers off as soon as it dried but Toady liked how hers looked and even though her nails broke and it wore off with the work she did at the Burns' house, she still did her best to keep her hands nice.

She had become close to Mrs. Burns, Irene. She did all of her personal care and Rayleen did the childcare and washing and they took turns making Mr. Burns his supper. Toady learned how Mrs. Burns liked things to be done in her home. She liked fresh flowers on the kitchen and dining room table. Even if they were just wildflowers and even if they were just dried weeds in the winter. She showed Toady how to arrange them. She wanted her under things and clothes handled only by Toady and she taught her how to fold them and how to use tissue paper in the drawers.

She liked Toady to bring her lunch and if she was in bed, it was always soup and toast. If she were up and around, it would be a white bread (store bought only) sandwich with butter and cheese and sweet pickles (store bought only) sliced beside the sandwich. Mrs. Burns liked to stay trim and she rarely ate more than a small portion. She did love the apple cake that Toady made for her and it was her only true indulgence. She liked the babies to always be dressed in little matching dresses that she had her mother send from the city. But she did not enjoy feeding them, diapering them, or holding them. Toady observed that they were more like dolls to her than real people.

Mrs. Burns had dolls too. She had a daybed in the spare bedroom that her parents had sent along with all the other furniture. It was covered in an opulent brocade, pinks, greens, and mauve. She had arranged on it twelve dolls that she had brought from her home. They were all porcelain faced with elaborate outfits, ranging from riding gear to an evening gown. Each was placed lovingly on the daybed by Mrs. Burns and she rotated the order that they were placed in once per week. No one touched the dolls but Mrs. Burns and when she was down, Toady was instructed on how the dolls should be arranged. Each doll was named and Toady made it her business to know all of their names. Evelyn, Maude, Henrietta, Ramona, Pearl, Yvette, Calendula, Angela, Myrna, Bonita, Lila and Portia. Once she knew their names and could refer to them by name, Mrs. Burns let her in on the pretend world in which these dolls were her friends and how each one accompanied her on different imaginary activities she participated in. For instance, Ramona was an excellent seamstress and whenever Mrs. Burns wanted to do some embroidery, which she actually did, Ramona was brought into the sitting room to sit in a chair beside her. But when Mrs. Burns was going riding (pretending), Calendula was brought in, wearing her riding outfit and was placed in the chair next to Mrs. Burns for an afternoon of "riding". That consisted of Mrs. Burns talking about riding and discussing the gait of her stead and the countryside around her.

Rayleen reported out to her mama and older sister that Mrs. Burns was looney and that Toady just encourages it by "tendin' them dolls is real folk". She hated the dolls and Toady had to warn her to never touch them. She would tease and say she dropped one down into the outhouse or that she had cut the hair off of one of them. But Rayleen mostly just steered clear of Mrs. Burns and put her full attention on taking care of those beautiful baby girls, Lily and Rose.

They were picture perfect little ones. They were at the toddling stage now and they were completely identical. Only Rayleen and Mr. Burns could really tell them apart. Rose had a little bit rounder eyes than Lily and you had to look closely, but you could see it. The little flowers, as their daddy called them, had soft curly blonde hair and light blue eyes, like a robin's egg. When he came home, they would run to greet him and he would pick them up in both arms. They loved their daddy and they loved their Rayleen, whom they called Ray-Ray. They knew better than to bother their mother. Somehow, as strange as it seems to most people, this unique family dynamic worked. The little girls had love all around them.

Toady was feeling in love. It was a restless feeling. Sometimes she felt so wound up she could not eat and then other times she sat and stared into nothingness, just feeling this strange new feeling. And there was shame in all of it because she was in love with someone who was married. And to make matters much more complex, she was in love with another woman. So, no matter how much her sisters teased her and no matter how much she wanted to tell them, it was impossible. Toady had never even heard that it was possible. She had never heard a word to describe it. Once her mama had told her that her great Uncle Pope had lived with another old man for years and that folk rumored, they "was just like an ol' married couple". But when Toady asked why they said that mama just chuckled and said, "what ya don't know won't hurt ya right now Toady".

The object of her love, Mrs. Burns, seemed oblivious to Toady's affection. She treated Toady like she had treated all the women who had cared for her since she was born. She was kind, willing to be taken care of, soft spoken, and perfectly suited to having a servant. Toady felt like everything she did for Mrs. Burns was a privilege and that was the greatest skill that Irene Burns possessed. She could charm people with her sweet southern womanliness. She could make her needs known and could always have them met. She could create her own world and inhabit it without longing for anything other than what she herself created. She was a true eccentric.

She had great affection for Toady, but she had not thought of it as love. She did enjoy

Toady's good looks and she noticed that unlike her sister Rayleen, Toady made more effort in taking care of herself. She complimented her on her hair and even taught her a new style that included using bobby pins for make pin curls. She even convinced Toady she should cut bangs for her and then she could curl them. The day Toady walked home with Rayleen with bangs and her hair in a low bun with auburn curls around her face, Rayleen had to stop and pee at the side of the road because she was laughing so hard. "Youense look so stupid! Who do ya think ya is, Toady? Youense look like an idiot!"

At home Mama was kinder and said she liked the new style. So did Lulu, but Biddy looked at her sister and said, "You ain't like Mrs. Burns Toady. Youense poor and stupid and cuttin' them there bangs don't mean nothin'." Leave it to Biddy to say just what was on her mind. But truth be told, it was on Mama's mind too. She worried about Toady; something was strange about that child. She was vulnerable in some way, unlike the other girls who tended to be tougher and frankly, meaner. Mama was keeping an eye on Toady.

CHAPTER 6

Chickens to Butcher

Lulu had just turned eighteen. She was starting to get pressure from everyone she knew about finding a husband and making some babies. She did not argue with them about it, but she knew she was not going that way. She had been making her mind up over the past few years, working for some money, having the freedom from household drudgery. She wanted more.

She had been talking to one of the salesmen, the fabric man, as Mr. Burns called him. He told her that there were jobs in clothing factories up north and also mill work down south. He talked about buses and trains carrying people all over, no need for your own vehicle, if you could make it to a city, get a job and then maybe room with some girls your own age. Or better yet, he chuckled, "marry one of them foreman and stop working all together." The store got the Kansas City Star Sunday edition on Wednesdays and she read the Help Wanted section each week, plotting a way to get somewhere where she could work and have a little apartment and see what being on her own really felt like.

It was during these days that life took a terrible turn for the worst for the Puckett family. Letty Anne became seriously ill. It was June and she had been butchering chickens that day. She had Arlan and the three younger girls helping her. The fire was stoked under the scalding kettle. Birdie was catching the chickens and pulling their neck through two nails hammered into the fence post by the barn. Then Biddy took the hatchet and lopped off their heads. Ticky dipped them in the scalding pot and mama plucked them. Arlan gutted them and then Biddy put them in the cold water trough in the shade. They had brought some ice blocks from Burn's General Store to cool down the trough. They were going to kill two dozen. Letty Anne could sell them all out of Burn's General and he only took a small cut off the top of her profits. This transaction had been negotiated by Lulu. Lulu had painted the signs that would be hung in the store window the next day advertising fresh layers, dressed and ready to put in the pot.

Butchering two dozen chickens was not too big of a chore. The kids were used to helping out with these tasks and it was easy to set up. But Letty Anne sat down about midday and asked Birdie to bring her a cup of cold water and a cold biscuit. That in itself was not unusual, but when Birdie returned, she found Mama laying on the ground, curled up in a ball of pain. Birdie screamed for her brother and sisters and everyone came to see what the commotion was about. They tried to help Mama up but she howled in pain. Arlan felt her head and Biddy said, "Get outta the way Arlan. Stupid boy, you don't know nothin' about helping sick women. Mama, kin you hear me, Mama?"

Mama moaned and said, "I got to get to the bed somehow. You kids gotta carry me. I feel like I cain't walk and my stomach is hurtin' real bad." Arlan put his eleven year old arms under Mama's arm pits and the three little girls lifted her middle and her feet. They all worked in unison, no one saying who should do what, just moving like they were one body. Pa came stumbling onto the porch as they passed by carrying Mama and he exclaimed, "What are youense doin' to your Mama?" Biddy threw daggers at him with her dark eyes and said,

"She is sick, Abel. Get outta the way."

They laid Mama down on her bed and she continued to moan and clutch at her middle. Abel sat by the bed and held her hand and Arlan took charge. "I will ride Spunk and get the doc. Ticky, you run into town and get Lulu. Biddy, you and Birdie keep working on the chickens. We is almost done. And Abel, you just sit your sorry ass there and tell Mama it's gonna be alright." As fast as he spoke, he was out the door, jumping bareback on Spunk and riding full speed to get the doc. Ticky took off running in her little bare feet all the way to her big sister Lulu at the store. Everything was happening fast.

The doctor and Lulu arrived about the same time. She had Rayleen with her as Mr. Burn's thought she should have one of the older girls there too. They ran from town and Lulu carried little Ticky on her shoulders. She was too worn out to run back.

Doctor Thomas had driven out in his Ford Model T Run About. He had bought it new and kept it running like a top. He was good under the hood of a car or a person, as folks liked to joke. As he pulled in Lulu was running up the driveway with Rayleen and Ticky and Arlan was hopping off of Spunk. Biddy and Birdie were standing on the porch with wet flour sack aprons, dirty with the days butchering. Lulu followed the doc into the house and the rest of the kids stayed outside.

The one room house was cool and dark and Doctor Thomas had to adjust his eyes when he stepped in. He heard Letty Anne's soft moans and walked to the corner of the big room and pulled back the muslin curtain. Arlan was sitting on an old wooden chair, looking as hang dog and useless as ever. Letty Anne was wound up in a ball of sweat with an old flannel sheet covering her. When the doc knelt beside her, he smelled the odor of cancer on her breath. He had smelled it so many times and he knew just what that sweet and sickly smell was followed by. As he examined Letty Anne, he began to softly ask her questions.

"Letty Anne, have you been feeling poorly?"

"Well, a little doc. I have lost my appetite and everythin' I eat hurts, but I know I have to... ohhh, it hurts when you push on me like that."

"Letty Anne, have you been using the outhouse regularly?"

"Well, I cain't eat much, so no, I just have waters coming out of me."

Doc turned to Lulu and asked "Have you known your Mama was not feeling well?"

Lulu shook her head no and said, "Mama is quiet doc. She has been doing everything like always. I guess she hasn't been eatin' much, but Mama is always eatin' kinda light..." Lulu suddenly felt selfish and foolish. How could Mama be this sick and no one know she was?

Abel spoke up and said, "Doc, she's been complainin' in her sleep about her gut hurtin'. When I tried to get her to talk about it, she just clams up."

Doctor Thomas pulled out a syringe and he told Letty Anne, "I'm gonna give you some rest now Letty Anne. You are gonna sleep for a while. That is the best thing to do now." He injected her with straight morphine and then asked Lulu to follow him out the back door. He stood looking at the run down barn and general disarray that was the Puckett's home. He knew all about Abel and how hard Letty Anne worked and how hard Abel worked at doing nothing. He looked at the pretty young woman in front of him, so serious and frightened. He sighed a couple of times and then said, "I think your Mama is dying."

Lulu stomped her foot in the dirt and said, "No she ain't! You is dead wrong about that!" She flung her arms around and pulled at her braid and she said repeatedly, "No, that is not true. No Doc, she just ate something bad. You don't just go dying over your first gut ache."

Doctor Thomas took Lulu by the shoulders and shook her gently. "Listen child, you are the only one I can depend on in this family to get this right. Your Mama is very sick. I think it's stomach cancer. She's been sick a while and she just fought back at it. She is a tough woman, just like you are Lulu. You gotta listen to me. She is going to get sicker and sicker and it is going to be very hard for all of you. I have medicine, but it won't stop some of what she has to go through. You listen to me now."

Then Doc wrapped his arms around Lulu and hugged her hard and when he released her, she was wiping tears from her eyes. He said, "I am going to take some samples of her blood and run some tests. Meanwhile, you just keep the kids quiet and fed and they can go in and sit by their Mama when she is sleeping, but they have to keep calm and quiet for her."

Lulu started to speak, but Doc spoke first. "I will stop by and talk to Mr. Burns. See if you can get your Mama's sister, Lutie, to come over and help out. Arlan can go get her. You all need to prepare for a few months of sickness ahead. And Lulu, someone needs to make her some soup out of that fresh chicken, but no meat in it. Just give her clear liquid from now on."

Lulu watched Doc go back into the house and she thought her feet were cemented into the ground. She could not move. She looked at the ridge above the house and she saw the trees leafed out and brilliant green. She saw the pile of chicken guts and feathers. She heard a mocking bird, mocking a crow. She felt the June heat rising up her legs and the June breeze blowing on her face. But all she could pay attention to was the big hole that was forming in her stomach. It was a big hole of grief and it felt like cold wind was blowing right through her and she could not stop it.

CHAPTER 7

Sickness

Things were figured out, as they always are, when a family has to rise to meet their circumstances. Lulu and Aunt Lutie were in charge of Mama's care. Rayleen stayed home and was the cook. Toady could not leave Mrs. Burns but she was earning money, so it was agreed she could continue. The little girls did laundry and Arlan took care of the chickens. Pa whittled and tried to tell Rayleen how to cook, until she threatened to smack him with a frying pan. Lulu went to the store for a few hours each day and gave Mr. Burns time to do his bookkeeping. It was all in hand.

Mama did suffer. Her tests came back-positive for cancer. Doc figured it had been growing in her stomach for at least six months. Aunt Lutie got Mama to talk about it more and she had been feeling sick for a long time, but she was hoping she was just moving into "the change." Lutie shook her head and held her little sister's hand. She had always worried about Letty Anne, since she had married Abel, but she never imagined putting her little sister in the grave long before it was her time.

The kids all had their own ways of looking at the situation. Arlan grew two inches and worked like a full grown man. He even built the outhouse and got Uncle Orvil and cousin Pod to help him dig the new hole. He made the outhouse a two seater and he found some screen at Uncle Orvil's and put in high windows on each side to let the breeze blow through. He wanted Mama to get to use it, but she could only use a chamber pot. Aunt Lutie walked her over to the back door one afternoon so she could see it and she burst into tears and said, "Arlan, you are the man of my dreams." Arlan never forgot that. He treasured those words his entire life.

Lulu did not think much about the future or anything other than work, keeping food on the table, and making sure Mama was as comfortable as possible. She left the kitchen and cooking in the capable hands of Rayleen. Rayleen was a master in the kitchen. She could create a meal out of damn near anything. No one got their biscuits to rise as high or their gravy as smooth. She devoted all her efforts to feeding the family. She made clear chicken stock soup for Mama and she baked a pineapple cake when Mr. Burns sent home a tin of canned pineapple for a treat. She did not complain and she did not miss being at Mrs. Burns with Toady and watching them play dolls while she worked. She imagined Toady was doing more work than she usually did and she was happy with that.

Toady was not so happy. She wanted to be at home with her family and help take care of everyone. But, Mrs. Burns, Irene, would cry when she said she needed to stay home for a few days to help her sisters. Irene would ask her to make the lemon bars that Rayleen made for her and then cry when they were not as good. Irene got in bed and would not come out for a week, wetting the sheets like a baby. Mr. Burns told Toady he would double her salary if she would just stick it out. Toady cried and asked him to please get some more help as she could not do it all. She told him the twins were suffering and missed Rayleen. Mr. Burns hired Missy May Palmer to help Toady and that started another chapter in Mr. Burn's life.

But back to Letty Anne and her illness. Her home was filled with love and sadness that summer. Everyone who loved her was close by. Her room had fresh wildflowers and wild mint in an old blue canning jar. Her bed had new sheets on it, made by Uncle Elmer's wife Aunt Bessie Mae. They were white with tiny blue flowers on them and a fresh new goose down pillow was brought over by one of the neighbor women. Cousin Darla sewed her two new night gowns out of soft muslin and embroidered little flowers on the sleeves.

Letty Anne drifted in and out of spaces in her mind. She thought she could smell things like fresh bread and apple pie, even when there was none in the house. She asked for biscuits with blackberry jam, but she could not eat them. The little girls sat in a row on the steps and ate the whole batch Rayleen had made, melting butter on them and dipping the spoon into the blackberry jam that was sitting in the jar between them.

Pa tried to have some serious conversations with Lulu and Lutie about when Letty Anne would be gone, but they told him to get his nose out of it and find some way to help out. One afternoon Biddy ran into Mama's corner of the house, pulled back the curtain and said, "Git out here Aunt Lutie! Youense ain't never gonna believe what's goin' on!"

Lutie followed her onto the front porch and lo and behold, Abel was repairing the fence that went around the old hog pen. They did not really need to have it repaired and no one was sure why he was doing it, but he was doing it. They did not have hogs at this time and when they did, they spent most of their time pasturing in the woods, eating acorns, until it was time to butcher them or the sows needed farrowing.

Abel had a hammer and nails and a saw and he looked like a normal man standing there with a pencil stuck in his overall pocket. Lutie shook her head and said, "Don't go makin' a big deal out of this Biddy. He's liable to quit doing it if you fuss. Just stay back and watch, cuz you may not see this e'er agin!" Biddy wanted to go over and throw some dirt clods at him and call him some names, but she listened to her Aunt Lutie, just like they all did. Her word was law.

Little Ticky suffered the most. She was just eight years old and she was the youngest. That meant, you might be overlooked when it came to serious work and over protected when you were trying to get someone to tell you the truth. But she was sneaky and she would hide behind the old bureau in Mama's corner of the house and listen to Doc talk to Aunt Lutie and Mama. She knew when the time for Mama to die was close and she did not tell the other kids, because she knew she was not supposed to hear it.

It was an afternoon in August. It was hot

and sticky out and Biddy and Birdie were taking turns waving a fan over Mama. When Doc came, they skittered out and he spoke very softly to Mama and Lutie. From her hiding place Ticky knew that he told them it would not be long and the suffering would be over. He gave Lutie a brown paper bag and told her how much and how often she was to give Mama whatever was inside of the bag. He was so tender when he talked to Mama and it make Little Ticky cry, but she did it silently so she could stay close by her Mama. When Doc left, she heard Mama telling Lutie how much she loved her and was thanking her for helping with the kids. Ticky could not hear it all, but she did hear her say, "They are gonna need to stick together for a while. I don't want them girls marrying off to some low life until they find themselves someone good. Better than Abel... You got to protect them for me Lutie."

Ticky thought about that and she decided she would not get married and she would just stay right where she was and take care of her brother and sisters. She was not old enough to get married, but she was sure she did not want to, ever, and she set her little heart against it, that day and forever.

Aunt Lutie broke the news to the kids over pork chops and boiled potatoes that evening. There had been plenty to eat this summer, in spite of the drought, and everyone kept dropping by good things like bacon, ham, chops, pies, fresh squirrel, and venison roast. No one went hungry, but Mama, of course. As Rayleen was putting a pork chop on each plate, Aunt Lutie gave them all a little speech. "Children. Your Mama is not long for this world. Doc says it will only be a few days and she will pass on to be with our Lord. Your Mama will go straight to heaven to live with the angels and she will sing in God's special choir. She will walk in fields of flowers and wear a beautiful white dress and her hair will have daisy chains fastened in it. She will be our special angel and when we miss her, we will bow our heads and pray and she will send love and comfort on her angel wings. Now, you all must be brave and you must be ready to let her go. You will go in one at a time and sit by her and near the end, you all can sit beside her and watch her pass on to the other shore."

She sounded like a preacher and no one spoke when she finished. They just dropped their heads and said Amen. It was the most that was ever said about her passing in one conversation. All other conversations were just bits and pieces and whispered or never spoken. Letty Anne was the foundation of the family and the only way they could go on was to imagine that she would always be with them.

And most of them believed that she was with them and it guided decisions they made for a long time.

Her funeral was simple. Uncle Orvil built a coffin for her and Aunt Lutie and Aunt Bessie Mae lined it with a soft blue fabric, stitched together into a quilted lining. They put bunches of wild sunflowers and wild asters on the top of the coffin. They buried her in the cemetery on the edge of Noble and Arlan made her a grave marker out of hickory wood. It was a cross and it said, "Letty Anne, Mother, Sister, Wife, and Daughter." In years to come, Lulu and Arlan put their money together and bought her a "real" headstone made of white marble and black granite. They let Abel be buried beside her, but he never did have a real headstone, just a wooden cross. He never was forgiven for being himself. He never won them over and he never did anything to deserve it.

The Aftermath

The family came home from the service. After the church dinner the pies and cakes were packed up to bring home with them. The last of the mourners expressed their condolences. Now it was time to face reality. When Lulu opened the door, she was hit by the faint smell of her mother's illness but the more pungent odor of the lavender and wild ginger that her Aunt Lutie had brewed and left on the stove. It softened the smell of death. They had already scrubbed the house top to bottom, opening the windows and doors to let fresh air flow through. They had washed and ironed Mama's sheets and the dress they buried her in. Lulu had made it for her in July.

She bought a fabric with blue forget-me-nots and used white eyelet to trim the collar. When she had helped Aunt Lutie put it on her Mama, all she could think about was wishing Mama could walk to church in it and Lulu could have picked some wildflowers and put them on her straw hat that she wore to church in summer.

Abel sat down in the rocker on the porch and was sullen. He did not have anything to say right now. Everyone was full and it was a Sunday, so they all settled into the house and yard with a sadness and laziness that followed them home from the cemetery. The younger girls took off the dresses that Lulu and Rayleen had made for them. They were yellow polka dot and they had been done in time for them to put them on and show Mama. She sighed and said they were the most beautiful little girls in the whole world. Biddy and Ticky fit the same pattern that Letty Anne had used many times for the older girls. For Birdie, Lulu had to use more fabric to fit her little round body.

They hung the dresses on wire hangers that Lulu got for them at the General Store. Usually they just hung their house dresses on nails, but Lulu wanted them to start taking better care of their clothes, knowing that she and Rayleen were going to be sewing them from now on.

Rayleen and Toady had chosen lavender fabric with pink roses. It was good fabric and

Rayleen and Lulu had taken great care making them. Toady took hers to Mrs. Burns house and showed her and she even complimented the fabric and added that Toady's auburn hair looked beautiful next to the lavender. She gave Toady a lavender ribbon and a small white patent leather bag with a new hanky in it. Toady proudly wore it to the funeral. She knew she was the prettiest girl there, but her heart was still at Mrs. Burns house, lost in her world of dolls and make believe.

Lulu had made herself a navy blue and white dress and used a new pattern. It was like the ones the fabric man had shown her that were being made in the factories "up north". It was tailored with boxy sleeves and she had ordered a navy blue belt to dress it up. Lulu was moving the Puckett girls into a new fashion, even though their house was old and the floors were dirt and the porch leaned. She also sewed a new shirt for Arlan out of the same navy blue fabric and made him a pair of pants from an old pair of Uncle Orvil's. All this was done in a week, so that Mama's family would look extra nice when they laid her to rest. Lulu and Rayleen had worked late into the night with kerosene lamps lighting up their work.

Soon the older girls found themselves sitting at the long table. No one was sitting in Mama's spot when Arlan came in and said, "Lulu, you need to sit at the head of the table now. I guess you is the Mama." Lulu knew this was true. She knew it the day Doc told her Mama was going to die. She was the Mama now and there was no getting out of it. From now on, she had to be here for her family and any thoughts she had about leaving or doing anything different than making sure this bunch was fed, clothed, and taken care of, were just ideas, not reality. She had cried quietly on her walks to the store and home again. Sometimes Toady would slip her arm in Lulu's and try to comfort her, but she was sad too.

Toady did not know what would happen to them, but she knew that it would depend on what Lulu could manage to do and that was it. Her eyes clouded with tears, but she had other worries in her heart too. She did not know how to deal with her feelings and she did not want to burden anyone with them. Plus, she was scared. She did not know what would become of someone who felt like she did about other women.

So, Lulu nodded at Arlan and said, "It kin wait till tomorrow. But, yes Arlan, I will be youense Mama until you get your skinny butts moved on."

Arlan looked at his three older sisters and he knew that he was still the man of the family. That old guy on the porch was just like a hound dog. You do not want to kick it; you have to feed it and it really does not do much of anything to help out. He kept thinking in his head, "Just throw the ole dog a bone."

In a while the three little girls came in and sat down too. Birdie had a big bouquet of wild asters in her hand and she put them in an empty jar from the cupboard. She then asked Lulu if she could have another piece of cake. Lulu said yes, they could all have some more cake. Toady brought the big jar of lemonade that Mrs. Caster had brought them and they had more cake and more lemonade.

So began the next chapter in the life of the Puckett Family. The seven children and their father would move forward together and do the best that they could, on poor soil, with rocky fields, dirt floors, no electricity, and not much money.

CHAPTER 9

Ira Burns

Ira Burns was a serious man. He had to be. Running the store and trying to take care of his wife and the twins was a full time job. He had become dependent on the Puckett's in a way he had not anticipated, but without the help of Lulu and Toady, he would be in far worse shape. After their mama died, he had talked Lulu back into full time work for him. He gave her the bookkeeping and ordering and spent more time running over to his place, which was only a five minute walk away, to check on how the twins were doing.

Lily and Rose were four years old now and they were surprisingly self-sufficient. He credited Rayleen for that and also the fact their mother was just like another child and forced them into figuring things out for themselves. He was grateful they had each other. They were darling little girls, with bouncy blonde curls and little heart shaped faces with twinkling blue eyes. That he credited Irene with as he himself was not especially handsome. He had a paunch of a belly, balding, and his nose was overly large. But he was smart and hardworking, so looks were of no concern in his life.

The twins were inseparable, as most twins are, and they were clever to boot. Lily was the bravest and she would try something and when it looked like she had it figured out, Rose would join in. One day he came home to find Lily sweeping the kitchen and Rose using the dustpan to pick up the crumbs. Lily said, "I can clean Papa and so can Rosie!"

Ira had tried to bring Rayleen back to work to take care of the twins, but she refused. She moved into the housekeeper role at home where her family needed her the most. He missed her good food and her tidy kitchen, but he understood. Instead he had hired on Missy May Palmer. Missy May was fourteen and she was capable in the kitchen, but she was hor-rible with the twins. They absolutely hated her and somehow got the idea to call her Pissy May. It drove her crazy and although Ira tried to stop them, they would call her that the minute he left the house. That was why he went home more often now, to be sure they had not done more than call her names.

One day Toady came tearing into the front door of the store and said, "Mr. Burns. You gotta come right now. The twins have been at it with Missy May and, well, you gotta come."

Mr. Burns did not even take off his apron and hollered back to Lulu, who was stocking shelves, that he would be back shortly. He trotted home, not able to keep up with Toady who could run fast on bare feet. When he threw open the front door all he could hear was Missy May screaming bloody murder. He ran into the kitchen to find her standing in the middle of the breakfast table, screaming in hysteria. All around her feet were big black snakes, writhing and turning on themselves. She was barefoot and they were crawling over her feet and she was so upset it looked like she had wet herself. He looked for the twins only to see their blonde heads dart past the screen door.

He first said, "Missy May, how in the hell did you git up there with them snakes? You jump off that table right now. Toady, help me to gather up these snakes. My God, what a fright you are makin' Missy May. Shut the hell up." He was picking up the big fat snakes, which were harmless, and chucking them out the back door. Missy May was paralyzed with fright and would not or could not stop screaming. Once the snakes were gone Mr. Burns yanked her off the table and shook her shoulders. "You stop that screamin'! You hear me?"

She started to blubber and her shoulders were still shuddering, but Toady brought her shoes to her and sat her down on a chair and put them on her. She said softly, "It's okay Missy. Them girls just got the best of ya, that's all. You just settle down now." She poured her a glass of iced tea and forced her to drink some of it as she patted her curly head of mousey brown hair and kept saying, "It's all right now Missy. You is all right now."

Mr. Burns sat down and held his head in his hands and said quietly, "Toady, would you mind walkin' Missy May home?"

She nodded yes and took Missy by the arm and walked out the back door. Mr. Burns heard her say, "Youense just git outta here and leave poor Missy alone. You are gonna get a whippin', but good."

Mr. Burns really did not have the energy to whip the twins right now. All he could think of was the mess his life was, married to a useless woman and raising two wild children, all the time working his hardest at the store. He put his head in hands again and a few tears fell out of his eyes. As he sat there, he heard the pitter patter of little feet behind him and two sets of little girl arms wrapped around his ample middle and Lily said, "Daddy, we love you, but we don't love Missy. We did a naughty thing, and we are ready to be whipped."

Rose uttered, "Uh-huh, we sure is Daddy."

Mr. Burns looked at his beautiful little girls and then he really started to cry. He cried hard and it scared the twins badly. It scared them enough that they tried much harder in the future not to be so naughty. But they had got what they wanted. Missy May never returned and Daddy had to start trying to find someone else to take care of his little flowers.

How Missy May ended up in the middle of the breakfast table with snakes around her feet, he never really knew, but he knew his girls and he knew that they could do just about anything together and that was the best thing about them.

Their mother did not say anything about the incident, but she told Toady later that she was proud of them and she too hated that "Pissy" May. All she said to Ira was, "Our girls are pretty good at taking care of themselves." He shook his head and left her sitting on her fainting couch.

Toady had to be devoted to Irene's care and Ira knew that. He had a mixture of feelings when it came to his wife. He resented her greatly and especially her family, but he still thought she was beautiful and she had given birth to his lovely daughters. He had stopped sleeping with her after they were born. Looking after her and twins, he felt the risk of more pregnancies was not worth it. He marveled at the fact her family rarely wrote to inquire about her.

One time one of her older sisters came by in a new car with her husband and without any notice decided they would stay for a few days. At that time he had both Puckett sisters and they managed, but he kept thinking after they left that surely, she would tell Irene's parents that she had not changed and that they needed to do something about it. Instead, he got a thank you note from Irene's parents that had a check for $200 in it, for the twins. They had never even met the twins, but it did not seem to bother them and Irene never asked to return home, so he just accepted it, just like he accepted his wife and her strange ailment.

Ira had no siblings himself and his parents were long gone. He only had a couple of cousins in Springfield and he never saw them. So, by default, the Puckett family really became his family. He knew they were good people and even if their father was a lazy no good rascal, Letty Anne had been a good mother and she had raised seven good kids. He felt good about keeping two of them employed and he always took care to send home extra groceries with

Arlan when he road in to pick up supplies for the family. He was a good man, that Ira.

Ira watched Lulu grow into a lovely woman and a capable employee. He always had a secret love for her but once she rebuffed him in the storeroom, he never tried to bother her again. But he wondered about her and why she did not have a boyfriend or why she was not in a hurry to marry. It could have made life so much easier for her, having a man to help her with the care of the family. But, then again, he remembered who her father was and thought it probably was not such a great idea to hitch yourself to just any man.

One day as they were closing up, he approached the subject. "Lulu, have you been thinking about what you might want to do about a family?"

Lulu chuckled and pulled down the shade at the front door. "I have a family, Mr. Burns."

"Yes, but about a family of your own. You could be keeping your own home with a good man."

Lulu took off her work apron and hung it on the hook behind the counter. She smoothed out the skirt of her dress and looked at Mr. Burns square in the eyes. "I appreciate your concern. But I like the way things is for me right now, thank ya."

She pulled on her gray wool coat and buttoned it up tight and said, "Good night. I will see youense in the mornin'."

Ira watched her walk down the road and his heart ached a little. He would have been a good husband to Lulu. He would have taken care of her and bought her a new coat and new shoes and nice furniture and she would have electricity and running water and make beautiful little babies. But, alas, he put on his coat and hat and walked home to the crazy family he had made instead.

CHAPTER 10

6 Feet Tall

Arlan was getting bigger by the day. He was on a growth spurt and got to be almost six feet tall by the time he was thirteen. He was skinny and awkward looking, but he was strong and he loved to work. His Uncle Orvil kept him busy on his place and then found him some work for different farmers in the area. He became a farm hand who worked for several different people at a time. He could do most of anything; carpentry, plowing, animal care, butchering, and horse breaking. He learned horse breaking at his Uncle's place. Uncle Orvil (or as Arlan referred to him, "Unc") liked horses. He bought and sold horses all the time. There was always a mare and a foal and/or a stallion on the place. He liked to have a good stallion for stud services and he taught Arlan how to handle those bigger and meaner horses. He told Arlan he had a knack for it as he showed no fear and the stallions respected that.

Arlan gave most of his money to Lulu for the household expenses. The kids were doing a good job at keeping the family afloat and she suggested Arlan open a bank account over in Springfield and keep some of his money in there. So, he did that. He road Spunk three hours, once a month, and put money in the Central Bank of the Ozarks. He would get out the bank book they had given him and look at the entries and marvel at the money he saved.

This just caused Arlan to hate his own father more. He could not believe that even after Letty Anne died that Abel was not trying to find a way to help the family to secure money. Abel took off at first, as they all thought he would, after Mama died, and he did not come back for one year. The kids thought maybe they had gotten rid of him forever and no one worried, but little Birdie. She would set a place for him at the table every night and no matter how much her brother and sisters teased her, she did it anyway.

Arlan saw his father first, again, when he came back after being gone for a year. He had just refreshed the laying boxes for the chickens and he was closing the chicken yard gate as Abel came walking down the road. He had on a new pair of overalls, still stiff from the sizing, and a new white shirt. His boots were new too and he had a haircut and a fresh shave. He was wearing a new fedora hat and he was whistling, just like he was a big shot coming down the road to gift them with his presence. Arlan balled up his fists and stepped out to meet him, standing at least 6 inches taller than the old man.

Abel spoke first, "Well hello boy! Youense has growed a foot since I last seen ya!"

Arlan crossed his arms over his own pair of old overalls and looked his father up and down. "What do you want, Abel?"

Abel took off his hat and held it and squinted at Arlan and said, "Now see here boy. That ain't no way to talk to yer Pa. I came home to see how youense is doin' and I don't mean no trouble. I even brought some money with me." Abel pulled out a wad of money from his front pocket and waived it at Arlan.

Arlan stood stock still and said, "You done spent it on yourself, Abel, by the look of them there britches and your fancy shirt."

Abel shook his head yes and said, "Well, a fella has to get new clothes sometime and I saved up plenty to bring home to youense. There's a $100 here." Again he waved the money toward Arlan.

Arlan turned away and walked toward the house and said over his shoulder, "Youense is gonna have to deal with Lulu concernin' that." He let the screen door slam behind him and he walked in to find Rayleen setting a fresh spice cake on the table. "You might want to put that up. Abel is back." Then he walked straight out the back door and left for Uncle Orvil's place.

After it seemed clear that Abel was not leaving, Arlan settled down and just went back to moving around his father without much notice. Arlan spent his time working. He was turning into an excellent farm hand. His days were busy and his bank account grew. He still looked at the picture of Mt. Adams and the blooming orchards in Washington and he vowed he would get there. He did not think he had to stay put to help his sisters forever. Afterall, Lulu, Toady, and Rayleen should be getting married one of these days. They were all of the marrying age, past it really, and he wondered why they did not look back at the boys at church who obviously had taken to them.

He thought that Lulu was just stubborn enough that she would not want a man in her life. She had always been the serious older sister, doing everything she needed to do and more. Toady seemed like a little girl to him even though she was going on twenty now. She took care of Mrs. Burns full time, and sometimes she even slept over at their house. Arlan asked her what she slept on and she said Mrs. Burns had a thing called a "fainting couch" and she would curl up on it. Arlan asked what you do with a fainting couch and Toady shook her head and said, "I think it is just to look pretty in her room. Her mama bought it for her. I ain't seen her faint on it, though."

Rayleen was the one he thought might try and marry. She was eighteen and she was a pretty woman. She had black hair and it was thick. Mama always said an Indian must have crossed the threshold because no one else in the family had that black shiny hair. She wore it in a braid down her back and she pinned it up off her neck in the hot sticky Missouri summer. She canned green beans and corn and she baked and she never complained. But when Bobby Parson asked her to walk with him after church, she said, "No thank ya. I gotta get home d'rectly and cook some Sunday dinner."

Bobby Parson asked every week for a while. He even asked if he could come home and taste her cooking, but she shook her head, no. Arlan teased her constantly about Bobby. She did not giggle or smile when he did that and she refused to say anything about it. Arlan went to Lulu and said, "Youense got to git Rayleen to marry, Lu. She is gittin' too old and it is bad enough that you and Toady is still old maids."

Lulu was sitting on the porch rocker the Sunday he said that, taking a well-deserved rest from responsibilities. She smiled at Arlan with a secret smile and said, "Arlan, what do you think we need a man for anyways?"

Arlan sat on the top step, still leaning north like the porch. He was chewing on a piece of jerky he had brought home from Uncle Orvil's place. He took a minute to answer and said, "For babies."

Lulu started laughing and said, "We got babies here! There are still three little girls that need us. What would we need more babies fer?"

Arlan thought for a bit and said, "Yer own babies. Not Mama's babies. Yer own little babies would be good."

Lulu chuckled and shook her head. "Boy, we are doin' just fine. Ifen Rayleen wants to git married, she is gonna git married. Nobody, no how, is tryin' to stop her. She got a mind of her own."

Arlan stared off into the blue sky and thought it was a shame that three good wives were sitting here, refusing to become mothers. But he also thought Lulu was right. Who would take care of the little girls? They were getting older. Biddy was twelve and acted like she was forty. Birdie was eleven and she was chubby and sweet and always had a little something in her pocket to chew on.

Ticky was ten and everyone knew what she

was thinking. It was the day after the funeral and they were all sitting down to eat their supper and Ticky stood on her chair and said, "Ever buddy listen up."

Ticky had been like a quiet little mouse all the time Mama was sick and sometimes Lulu would find her hiding behind Mama's old bureau, sucking her thumb and holding her rag doll. Ticky had never stood on a chair and demanded their attention. So, naturally, they all put down their forks and looked at her. She looked so tiny and skinny and her little knees were scraped from playing in the barn and in the woods. Her hair was in braids but it would never stay in them and it was poking out and fly away around her face. She smoothed it back and said, "Mama don't want none of youense to git married. She said there is too many no-good men out there and she said to watch out. So, I am tellin' ya, I ain't gittin' married and I am gonna stay right here and Arlan, you kin be my pretend husband."

Of course the little girls giggled and so did Rayleen. Lulu stayed serious and Arlan said, "No way am I yer pretend nothin'!"

Abel had not run off yet and he said, "Ticky, yer mama never meant them to stay old maids. She just wanted them to do some careful pickin' afore they git hitched."

"Like she done, is that what you mean Abel?"

That was Biddy. She never let Abel off the hook.

Abel started to argue and Lulu interrupted. She said, "Ticky, youense can stay here long as ya like. Ifen you change yer mind, I know a good man is out there for ya."

Ticky sat down, stuck her tongue out at Arlan and said, "Thank ya Lulu."

That conversation was an omen, or so Arlan thought. As it turned out over time, of the girls, only Biddy and Birdie ever married. He did get married, but not to anyone from Missouri. But time passes before we are ready for that part of the story.

CHAPTER 11

Abel

Arlan was only fifteen when World War II started. He could not go off to war like cousin Pod and Basil and nearly every other boy in their part of the Missouri Ozarks. They all road the train to St. Louis. When the train pulled out of the station in Ava, people from all around the area were standing by to send them off. Arlan wanted to go, of course, but Uncle Orvil and Lulu kept telling him how much everyone was going to need a good farm hand now that all the young men had up and gone to war. He hopped up on his new horse Coyote (Spunk was getting too old for long rides) and road back home feeling left out and useless.

When he got home Abel was sitting on the

porch and he did not look up at Arlan or try to say anything to him. He had his head down and tobacco juice was rolling down his whiskers. Arlan walked up on the porch to get a better look at him and asked, "What's wrong with ya Abel?"

Abel shook his head like it was not anything, but Arlan knew he was out of sorts. Not that he cared much about Abel and his feelings or what he was up to these days, but something had changed. He kept an eye on Abel for a few days and asked Lulu what she thought was going on. She just shrugged her shoulders and told him she just did not have time for Abel and his problems. She was worried about keeping her job and how to deal with all the shortages that folks said were coming and how the store was going to keep up. She took one look at Abel and just shook her head. He looked as lazy as ever.

Arlan decided he would go and talk to his father's brother, Uncle Elmer. One afternoon when he had a free couple of hours, he rode Coyote over to Uncle Elmer and Aunt Bessie May's place. Every time he came up on their house, he was always taken back by the difference between Elmer Puckett's place and Abel Puckett's place. You would not think they were from the same family. Uncle Elmer had a house painted white with green trim. It had pretty shutters that he had made, painted green and with a star cut in the center of each one. The screen door was painted green too and it hung nice and straight and the screens were tight and clean. The porch was railed and had nice wooden steps to match. Aunt Bessie May had a flower bed on both sides of the stairs that was always planted with zinnias and asters in the summer and pansies and violets in the spring.

The barn was straight and did not lean. It was painted barn red and it had a matching chicken coop between it and the house. The garden was fenced in to keep the deer out and Aunt Bessie put the chicken droppings in it every fall to make it good and rich. Uncle Elmer had electricity, indoor plumbing and wooden floors.

Elmer and Bessie never had children. They tried and there had been two that made it a few months in the womb and after that they could not even get one to start, as Mama always said. But they had put their time and effort and money into making their place into a little piece of heaven. Uncle Elmer always had a good passel of hogs and he worked for the railroad. Aunt Bessie had nice things and she was an excellent baker. She made cakes for weddings and her pies were always the first to go at church bake sales.

Arlan loved to visit them. The house had clear paned windows and it always was clean and smelled good. Today Uncle Elmer was home preparing for hog farrowing. When Arlan walked in he said, "Just the man I wanted to see! Gettin' ready to farrow pigs, son. Youense want to help out? Good for some bucks and Aunt Bessie's cookin'? We'll be startin' tomorra."

Arlan grinned. He knew Uncle Elmer was aware that he was always working and he knew he already had some of the cousins from Bessie's side of the family coming to help him. Aunt Bessie motioned for him to sit down at the table. He ran his hand over the oil cloth, not sticky, and printed with bunches of grapes. A piece of apple pie was placed in front of him with big a glass of cold milk, before he could even say a word. Aunt Bessie was working on something over the stove and Uncle Elmer sat down at the head of the table. "How's things over at yer place, Arlan?"

Arlan talked about the weather, the chickens, his sisters, slow and probably sounding a lot older than fifteen, but he was the man in his house and he wanted Uncle Elmer to see him that way. When he finally spoke of Abel, it was hard to figure out what to say. Uncle Elmer helped out by saying, "How's that lazy no-good brother of mine"?

"Well, I don't know, Unc. He's been actin' peculiar. He ain't sassin' the girls or houndin' me like he usually does. He ain't eatin' much and just looks more and more like an ol' hound dog, sittin' on that porch with his head hung down. It's pathetic."

Elmer listened carefully, nodding his head and then he said, "That don't sound nothin' like Abel. That fool has always had somethin' to say."

Aunt Bessie stepped over and asked Arlan, "Has he walked into Noble lately, for tobacco or anythin'?

Arlan shook his head no. Then he said, "He ain't goin' no where or sayin' nothin'. It's kind of spooky."

Uncle Elmer sighed and said, "I'm gonna come over d'rectly and bring him back to our place for some supper. I'll see what he has to say then."

Arlan thanked his Uncle and praised his Aunt's pie and sat and enjoyed the cozy kitchen for a bit longer. "Well, gotta git. I am due over to Roy Hubbard's to help him finish up his new hog pen. Thank ya much, Unc. 'Preciate it."

As Arlan rode a way, he turned and looked back at Uncle Elmer's farm. He wanted that very farm, but he wanted it sitting in the middle of an apple orchard, facing that big Mt. Adams out in Washington State. He thought he would paint his house that same color and make a flower bed for his wife, just like Aunt Bessie had. He nudged Coyote into a trot and headed to the Hubbard's place.

Uncle Elmer did go and pick up Abel. He brought along a ham and one of Bessie's fresh loaves of bread. He came in his old wagon, just because he knew Abel was more comfortable in a wagon than in a motor car. He told his brother he needed some help with farrowing the sows and said he would not take no for an answer. Then there was also butchering and he needed help with that too. Abel climbed up beside him on the wagon seat and never said a word. Very strange because Abel was a talker and he always had something or other to say. You would have thought he was an educated man the way he liked to pontificate on any subject, whether he knew anything about it or not. But this day he rode silently along and Elmer kept looking at him sideways, wondering just what had hit him.

The brothers did not talk about feelings or anything like that ever. So today Elmer tried to bait Abel into talking about hogs, since he knew Abel thought he knew everything about everything. He said, "Well Abel, that old sow, Charlotte, she ain't lookin' so good today. I think she ain't got many more litters in her. What do ya think?"

Abel spit his chew out and said, "Dunno know."

Elmer tried again, "Do youense think she is just woed (worn) out or what?"

Abel shook his head and looked down. Elmer got exasperated and said, "God damnit Abel, what the hell? You talk more than anyone I know! What's ailin' you?"

Abel shuffled in the wagon seat and said, "Cain't go to war Elmer."

Elmer said, "What? Ya cain't go to war? What the hell Abel? You is over forty five and you ain't ever been worth a damn at doin' anythin'! Go to war? They ain't gonna take ya to war Abe."

Abel spit again and said, "I knowed that, but it don't mean I don't wish I could go. I seen Basil and Pod goin' and all them other boys and I just thought, it might be time I did somethin' about somethin'. I don't know..."

Elmer shook his head and sighed. He said, "You ain't done nothin' about yer family. What you wanna go off to war fer?"

Abel truly looked unhappy and he shook his head and said, "I jes don't know Elmer. I jes feel like I could do somethin' for the war. I knowed I is useless to my family. I knowed that and now they all don't even need me or care if I am dead or alive. I think they would like me to be dead and gone, just like Letty Anne. None of 'em has a lick of respect for me. I feel like I'm the old family dog, just kicked aside."

Elmer had so much to say, but he had never

heard his brother say this much about anything personal, so he let his words sink in for a bit before he replied. He closed his eyes for a second and tried to see what Abel was saying, but it just seemed unreasonable. When had Abel ever cared about who needed him or who loved him? Maybe Letty Anne, he loved her, but he left her all the time. Why? No one ever knew just where he would go either and what kind of work he did, always coming back with some cash and new clothes. Abel was a mystery to him. He was nothing like any of his family. Elmer and Abel's ma and pa had been good people, hardworking, even though his pa was a bit of a lazy one too, but they always took care of their family. Even Abel seemed okay when he was a young man. He took care of Letty Anne for the first few years, but after Rayleen was born, bad luck and bad judgement got the better of him.

The truth was that Abel discovered gambling about that time. First it was just card playing, innocently, with friends. Then he heard about a game over in Ava where they were betting seriously and even a horse or worse yet, a farm, had passed hands. He had won nearly every game with the first group of men, who were just playing for pennies or tobacco or sometimes a sack of grain. He found he could remember the cards played and he had a knack for a poker face. His poker face was what some would call "just talkin' bull shit all the time". He kept up a steady stream of nonsense that distracted the other players. It worked fine in most circles, but not at the high level games he eventually got into.

One day he hitched a ride to Ava with his brother Elmer and he was gone for about a week. He came home with some material for Letty Anne and a pocket watch for him and a new ax for all of them. Letty Anne asked how he got them and he just chuckled and said, "I worked fer 'em Letty Anne." Letty Anne looked him over. His bull shit did not work on her. She shook her head and went back to her work, wondering just what he was doing to get those things. The material was good high thread count cotton and dyed a rich blue. The pocket watch looked like someone else had used it often and so did the ax. She wondered if he stole them, but she had never known him to do that.

It was not long after that the one of the fellows he gambled with in Ava told him about St. Louis and the amount of money to be had up there. That was the first time he took off. He hitched rides until he got there. He slept wherever he could find a corner. He lurked and haunted every gambling establishment he could find. He would take some day work and live in one of the flop house hotels until he could get enough to get in on a game. It was about a year of this before he got the courage to bet the higher stakes, but he had some luck and with that came more money and a room at a good hotel and some fine clothes, so he did not always look like such a hillbilly.

Sometimes old overalls and a scrunched up hat was his uniform. They threw the other players off, thinking he was stupid and had no experience with the big games. He made it all work for him and when he would get a big pay load, he would think about going home but the lure of the game was too strong. He would vow to save up some of the winnings, but most of it went back to the tables.

Abel was like a chameleon. He adjusted to whatever the circumstances of the current game called for. Dressed up as "fancified" for one game and another across town called for work clothes, but not overalls, and a passion for spitting chew in spittoons. Another one it worked just to be still and be dressed in a suit and nod and watch, but never revealing that you were a hillbilly from the Missouri Ozarks. He was a master of disguise there and sometimes he wished Letty Anne could see how skilled he was at dropping in and out of situations.

At times Abel was tempted by the prostitutes, but he kept his faith with Letty Anne. He would dream of her at night and yearn to go home to her, but the sickness of gambling would keep him in St. Louis. He knew every dark corner of that city after his first stay and when he went home to Letty Anne, it was only because there was a price on his head for some debts he owed and the men he owed them to were dangerous. So, he snuck out of the city and went back home, empty handed, except for the old nag he won off some old man in Springfield.

Letty Anne was strangely in love with Abel, but she regarded him by the time he left her for years, as a lost child of hers, one she loved, but one she had to move on from and bury the sorrow it caused her. When he returned, each time, she thought she might not love him anymore, but he was like a pair of old shoes that still fit, even if the water seeps in when you step in a puddle. She tolerated Abel and to her amazement, he thought that was just enough to keep him in her bed.

After he returned when the little girls were small, she never did let him have relations with her again. She would let him cuddle and tell her how much he loved her, but only in the dark in their bed. But when he wanted to do more, she kicked him like a mule and told him those privileges left the last time he did.

What Abel's kids never knew was that the whole time he stayed home and rocked and talked, he was fighting a demon of addiction.

They did not know it and they never would. If he was not so useless as a wage earner, he might even have garnered the affections of some of them other than Birdie. But they only knew him as the man who sat and did nothing, not the man who sat and fought his urge to leave for the card table every day that he stayed there.

You might think a gambler could have never done what Abel did, not playing for years at a time. But you did not know a man like Abel. He had a strange morality. He did not cheat on his wife. He did not take anything from the farm or the family to gamble. He earned all the money he used for gambling away from the farm. He felt almost pious in these practices. He was not hateful and he did love his wife and kids. He did not drink moonshine or whiskey and if he drank a beer, it had a purpose, like keeping the suspicious fellow gambler thinking he was an old drunk. Abel did not feel so bad about himself.

But the war made him feel like he would never fully do his part as a man. Elmer, who had always suspected what Abel did when he was gone, could not fathom that this would make his brother feel useless. He could not fathom those years of lassitude and perverse waste of manhood had not done that to him. But he too, like Letty Anne, had a soft spot for his little brother and to cheer him up he kept him over at his place working with the sows for a while. Then Abel up and disappeared and only came home one more time, to die.

CHAPTER 12

War Years

As time went on, everyone adjusted to what being in a war meant. It meant shortages of many things, but it was worse for people who needed gasoline and could not grow their own food. The Puckett family had most of what they needed and they did not own a car. They had a hard time getting coffee and sugar, but they still had molasses for baking and chicory for making a drink almost like coffee.

Lulu handled the ration books down at the store and set up a system for Mr. Burns to deal with it. She also bargained with the salesman and would bring in some of the things that were hard to come by in other places. She liked the idea of a shortage. She saw it as a challenge for the business and she figured out all kinds of ways to keep the shelves stocked. She also felt for the customers who lost the men to work the farms due to the war. She felt for the mothers and widows who came in and picked up mail at the post office next door and then sat down on the benches in front of the store to cry at the loss of a loved one or to smile as they read a letter from Europe from one of their kin.

Cousin Pod made it through the war, but his little brother Basil did not. He died in a field of mud in France, blown clear in half by a tank. The whole family gathered on the platform at the train station to carry his casket to the cemetery behind Rocky Point Baptist Church, not far from Letty Anne's plot. Uncle Orvil and Aunt Lutie held hands and leaned on each other as the preacher read the sermon, laying their dear boy to rest. Pod could not come home, but little Darla was still at home and she cried so hard and could not be consoled. She was two years younger than Basil and he had been her best playmate and pal as they grew up. Pod had always been the responsible one, but Basil was silly and wild and always kept everyone laughing. Things would never be the same for their family without Basil. He was only nineteen when he died.

They were not alone in loss and many a young man did not return to the Missouri

Ozarks. Some came home without a leg or an arm or one eye gone. The war wounds were horrendous. Some came home physically intact, but with minds that wandered back to the war unexpectedly and with bad consequences. Some took up drinking or wife beating. Some took off after they got home and disappeared into the hills in Arkansas, unable to cope.

Cousin Pod came back miraculously whole. He had made it through the war and it was not that he had not had a horrendous experience that could have messed him up for life. He had been a medic, trying to help dying men all day each day. He saw the worst of the wounds and had pushed the guts back into many a soldier as they screamed for their mother. But Pod was a man of steel. He always had been. He was tough as nails, strong as an ox, and he had an even temper.

Arlan was kept extremely busy helping people and often without pay. A strong young man was needed by so many folks who lost their own strong young men to the war. He worked for Uncle Orvil and Aunt Lutie often. With both boys gone there was plenty of work that could not be done just by Uncle Orvil. He paid Arlan often with food and he fed his horse for him regularly. Arlan loved Uncle Orvil and Aunt Lutie and he would have helped them for no pay any time. But Uncle Orvil knew everyone in their part of the world and he was always sending Arlan off to this one and that one to help with cutting hay, digging the spuds, building a fence, plowing a field, mending a porch, whatever they needed.

Arlan grew bigger and stronger, and even when he could have signed up for the war he did not go because he had become so vital to the health and wellbeing of his own community. The draft did not affect him until he turned twenty one and by then the war was over. So he stayed out of the war and did all he could to make up for it. He became well known by many people and was considered a good man. Lulu heard more than one farmer sitting on the bench out front talking about him. They said things like, "That Arlan Puckett...he's a good 'en. Ain't nothin' like that worthless old man of his. You should see him toting bales of hay off them wagons, sometimes two at a time! He is pure muscle that boy."

Lulu smiled and felt such pride in her brother. She wished her mama could have seen what a man he had grown into. He was six foot and two inches tall. His back was broad and his arms rippled with muscle. He had a shock of black hair that she kept trimmed up for him and he had grown a thick black beard. His eyes were sparkling blue and he could have his pick of girls, but he seemed to be saving himself for something. Not many people knew what that was, but Lulu knew it was for an orchard in Washington State in the great Yakima Valley where the water flowed from the Cascade mountains into canals, every year, no drought and no doubt you could grow a good crop in that hot desert sun.

Rayleen was still the chief cook, gardener and minded the hens. She had a deep and abiding love for Missouri. Not that she had ever been anywhere else, but she felt akin to it all. She liked the rolling hills, the deep hollers, the creeks that dried up in August and rushed in with water in March. She loved the wild black-berries and picked them endlessly. She filled jar after jar with the deep purple jam and pie filling and dried them for cobblers in the winter. Her garden was her pride and it was even better than Mama's had been. She had a knack for growing things and she could cut a switch off a Rose of Sharon bush, stick it in the ground and have a bush by the next spring. She grew to-matoes that were big and juicy. Her green bean vines were covered and she canned them as fast as she could pick them. Rayleen was fond of flowers and she dug a big flower bed on each side of the porch and down the house. She grew cone flowers, columbines, coreopsis and dug wild hyacinths to fill out the beds. She asked Lulu to try to get seeds for some other flowers and once she could get dahlias, she made a row of dahlias in the garden, right beside a row of zinnias.

She helped turn the old farm into a nicer place. She got Arlan to rebuild the porch. She hauled off the junk in the yard. She painted the outside of the house and got Lulu to agree with putting in a wood floor and even some linoleum on top of the wood in the kitchen. The farm transformed and everyone who road past said something nice to her about how good things were looking. Rayleen only wished her mama had been able to have it so nice, but she always felt her beside her at the stove when she cooked, gathering the eggs, digging in the dirt. She felt that her mama had never really left the farm and so each thing she did she felt her mama's hand on her shoulder, giving her a little squeeze of approval.

Ticky was Rayleen's little shadow. She followed her everywhere and was learning to do everything just like Rayleen. They sent her to school, along with Biddy and Birdie, but she really hated it and had many "tummy aches" when it came time to walk to the little schoolhouse by the church. Rayleen felt sorry for her, so when she stayed home, she taught her reading, writing and math. Ticky was smart, but she was a little withdrawn from others. She never really got over Mama dying. She was always a little lost after that and Rayleen tried to fill in the void for her.

Ticky liked to play alone anyway. She would wander in the woods around the house and spy fairies and talk to bunnies and imagine she could fly. She told elaborate stories to Rayleen about her make believe world and her older sister listened with rapt attention. She started calling Ticky, Little Sprite, and that was Ticky's second nickname. No one ever did call her Pauline and half the family called her Ticky and the older girls called her Sprite. That was the way with their family. Nicknames were for life, no matter how you got one.

Biddy and Birdie still did everything together and Biddy always came up with the ideas. When they turned sixteen and fifteen, she decided they need to get engaged to someone and plan their escape from the Missouri Ozarks. Biddy sat Birdie down and made a list of some of the younger boys that were still around and not off in the war. She instructed Birdie on how to fix herself up for attracting one of these boys. "First, stop eatin' ever thing that comes in front of youense. You ain't gonna git a man if you cain't fit into a perty dress, Birdie. Put down that damn biscuit!"

Biddy knew who she was going to pursue. His name was Bill Butters. He was eighteen and he was heading to the war in a couple of months, so she had to move fast. It was not hard for Bill Butters to fall for Biddy. She was a pretty girl, robust and rosy cheeked. Her hair was auburn like Toady's and thick as a rope. She kept it long and had a knack for pinning it up, curling it, or fixing it in styles from the magazines that Toady brought home from Mrs. Burn's house. She was an excellent seamstress. The best in the family. She could look a dress over and make it with no pattern. She loved to wear yellow. She said it was her signature color, as she thought it made her auburn hair really shine.

Bill Butters did not know what hit him. He fell head over heels for Biddy and the day he left for the war she had an opal engagement ring (from his Granny) on her finger and as she kissed him good-bye, she ordered him to come home alive and they could get married and move to Kansas City. She handed him a little leather folding picture frame and there was two pictures of her that she had gone all the way to Springfield to have taken. She looked beautiful and she knew it and Bill Butters teared up, kissed her hard, and said, "I'll be back Biddy."

Birdie was more challenging because she did not necessarily think that at fifteen, she had to be ready. Biddy reminded her that their own mama had been very young when she got married. But she also said, "Youense is not marryin' some ole coot like Mama did. We is gonna find you someone proper." Birdie sighed and eyed the last piece of apple cake on the plate and Biddy snatched it away and hollered for Ticky to come and get it.

Biddy did not try to mess with Ticky. She thought her little sister was strange and she had a feeling she was never going to leave home. She was right. So, she poured her energy into Birdie and she found her the perfect match. Willard Caster, little brother of Arlan's old tormentors. Willard was shy like Birdie and he had a sweet tooth and was round in his striped overalls. Biddy talked him into coming over after church and have some dinner with the family. Willard was quite uncomfortable at that dinner, his head dropped down most of the meal. Arlan asked after his "bastard brothers", which was not helpful and Biddy let Arlan have it later that day.

But after dinner, Biddy sent Willard and Birdie out to the porch and ordered Ticky to take them each out a big slice of blackberry pie and then "git the hell outta there". Willard kept coming around and Birdie thought he was "so cute" and he thought Birdie was "perfect", as he told his mama. So, Biddy got that arranged and she told Birdie and Willard that if they wanted to, they could move up north to Kansas City with her and Bill when he got home.

Willard and Birdie at that point in time had fallen so deep in love, she could have said they should live in a tree house in Florida and they would have agreed. It was a good spring for all of them that year. The war casualties were a little lighter, mostly because so many of the boys had perished. There was talk of an end to the war and although the war was real to them, there were so many things that had not changed in their world. They passed their days in much the same way that their parents had. There were more cars, but not as many as you would think. There was now a telephone at the store, but no one had one in their houses, except Mr. Burns.

The shortages were a little easier on them because they were growing most of what they ate, and besides, their diet had not changed since way back when their families moved there from Virginia. Everyday included dried beans cooked in pork fat, cornbread, biscuits, bacon or ham, potatoes, onions and fresh vegetables in summer. Most food was fried or had bacon grease as part of the recipe. No one was used to candy or anything sweet that was bought in a store, except for an occasional hard candy. They ate fried apple pies and molasses cakes and when they got some ginger, they liked gingerbread. Green beans were cooked long and slow with a slice of salt pork for flavoring. They ate some fried chicken when they butchered a hen or two. They liked it with dumplings too and sometimes home-made noodles in chicken broth. All that was still available to them during the war. So they thrived and except for the losses of the young men, they moved through the war years with a kind of grace that comes from living simply.

CHAPTER 13

Strange Bedfellows

The only one of the family who was not feeling very secure with their life was poor Toady. Toady was still tied to caring for Mrs. Burns. She did not want to leave her, but she could not see what her future would be if she stayed. Irene had become more dependent on her than ever.

The twins were eight years old and they went to school every day and they had grown into nice girls. Their father had finally found the right caretaker for them after the Missy May disaster. He hired Ruby who was from one of the black families that lived just on the outskirts of Noble. Ruby was a strong person. When she took the job, she was just fifteen and she had grown up with a house full of brothers and two little white girls with tempers were not anything she could not handle. In fact, Mr. Burns paid her an extraordinary amount for her work, begging her to stay, and as it turned out, Ruby was there until the girls left for the University of Missouri when they were eighteen. So for fourteen years, they lived and learned with Ruby Porter and they were the prettiest and best mannered girls for fifty miles around because of it.

But back to Toady. She was truly a beauty at twenty three and everyone had just given up on her ever getting her to agreeing to get married or take a different job. Rayleen talked with Lulu about it often and said she really felt that Toady had a peculiar relationship with Mrs. Burns. "It ain't right, Lulu. That woman is crazy and our perty sister is just wastin' away, playin' dolls with her and combin' her hair and whatever they is doin'. It just ain't right."

Lulu agreed, but she worked with Mr. Burns every day and she knew that someone had to take care of his wife or his household would become too chaotic. She had even talked to Mr. Burns about it one day when they had closed up and were getting ready to go home. "Mr. Burns, how long do ya think youense is gonna need Toady workin' for ya?"

Mr. Burns stopped in front of the counter and

leaned against it with a sigh. Lulu thought he looked like an old and tired man right then, but she knew he was only in his forties. He wiped his face with that motion that older men use where they take their whole hand and run it across their face and then rest it on their chin. Then he said, "I wish I knew, Lulu. I wish I knew. It is hard to say. I mean, I don't have any idea if she can do it without help. I really don't..."

"It is jest that Toady is gettin' older and maybe she should be thinkin' of doin' somethin' else. I jest worry about her gettin' stuck, you know, stuck."

Mr. Burns nodded in agreement and then he said, "She and Irene are mighty close Lulu. I don't know what ya call it, but I think they are in love in some way."

Lulu spun around and frowned and said, "That ain't no way to talk Mr. Burns. They ain't in love. Jest that Irene can't take care of herself and Toady, she's a softy, you know, she don't wanna hurt her by leavin'."

Mr. Burns sighed and said, "Lulu, you talk to Toady and ifen she is ready to leave, you just tell me and I will explain it to Irene. I didn't mean to offend you Lulu."

Lulu felt so sorry for Mr. Burns right then. He looked so sad and dejected and he really had not offended her because she knew full well that her little sister was in love with Mrs. Burns in a very unnatural way. She could see it on her face whenever she talked about Irene and she knew that many nights when she did not walk home with Lulu, it was because she just did not want to leave Irene. In fact, she wondered if they were going to ask Toady to live there soon.

She walked over to Mr. Burns and she patted his shoulder and said, "Not offended Mr. Burns. I will have a talk with Toady, but like as not, she'll wanna stay with Irene. I'll see youense tomorra."

Mr. Burns looked at her and his eyes were welling up with tears. He loved Lulu, but she would never return his love. And maybe his wife loved another woman and maybe he had got swindled when he married her, but he was lost regarding what he could do about it. He did not want to upset his daughters. They were his pride and joy and the best thing he ever had a part in and he just did not want to do anything that would make life stranger or harder for them.

Lulu walked home alone that night and thought about how she could find a way to talk to Toady about the future. She dreaded it. But she knew Mama would want her to do something about what was going on over there. She tried to ask Mama as she walked home, praying as she plodded home, listening and worrying all the way. Sometimes she asked Mama for help and sometimes she thought she got a sign from her. So she looked up in the trees and scanned the clouds and listened to the birds, just hoping for a sign. But nothing happened.

When she got home Rayleen had made a nice stew with some meat that Uncle Elmer had brought over and Ticky had made a big pan of biscuits. Everyone was there that night, except Toady who had stayed with Mrs. Burns again. As they sat around the table, talking and sharing stories, and passing the biscuits and the molasses and butter, Lulu looked at all of them and got her answer and she figured it was directly from Mama.

They were strong. They were Pucketts. They made their own way and each of them was choosing what that was going to be. She and Rayleen did not want to marry, Arlan had big dreams of going west, Biddy and Birdie were going to be married and Lulu knew full well they would leave and head to the city. Ticky was sticking with Lulu and Rayleen and no amount of persuading would change that.

So why shouldn't Toady get to choose? So what if she was in a "unspoken" love affair. So what if she loved a lunatic. It was her life and right then and there, Lulu knew she would not interfere with Toady's plans. She would ask her what she wanted and then she would help her get it, even if she wanted to live with Irene

Burns the rest of her life. She knew she had got her answer from Mama.

So, one afternoon a few weeks later, on a Sunday, Lulu asked Toady to walk with her over to Uncle Orvil and Aunt Lutie's house to deliver a pie that Rayleen had baked for them. Rayleen said she would come too, but Lulu looked at her with a raised eyebrow and said, "I reckon I would like walkin' with Toady alone today." Rayleen understood. She packed the pie in her favorite "pie carrier", a wicker basket that Mama had fixed up for carrying pies. She put a flour sack tea towel around it and latched the lid on it for safe carrying.

Lulu carried the pie in one hand and looped her other arm through Toady's. They had been walking that way all their lives, arm and arm, from little girls picking blackberries to big girls going off to work. When they were far enough away from the house Lulu said, "Toady, do youense remember Audie and Wilson, them two old men over by Ava?"

"Sure do. 'Member, Mama used to make us take them firewood in that ol' wheelbarrow? She said they was gittin' too old fer choppin' wood no more."

"Yeah, and 'member how they always wore matchin' shirts and we used to act up and laugh about it when we came home and Mama told us she would switch us?"

"Yep, I 'member. Did them ol' boys die?"

"Oh yeah, a few year ago. But, you know, them ol' boys was like they was married. Did you knowed that?"

Toady squirmed out of Lulu's grip and said, "Na, they weren't married."

Lulu, sat down on a tree stump next to the path and said, "Yes they was, in their hearts. And Mama said it was all right with her, cuz they never bothered nobody and they was always kind."

Toady frowned at her and kicked at the dirt. "Yeah, well, Mama was good like that. She never talked bad about no one."

Lulu said, "She loved us all and she still does. She loves us no matter who we love or what we wanna do, long as we is kind to people and work hard."

Toady nodded her head and said, "Mama knew how I felt afore she died. She told me it was gonna be all right."

Lulu looked hard at her sister and said, "She did?"

Toady said, "I ain't got no reason to lie 'bout it Lulu!"

Lulu said quickly, "I knowed that. Well, I am glad, real glad. You jest know that I am like Mama. You do what you wanna do Toady and that will be just fine."

Toady giggled and said, "Let's get over to

Aunt Lutie's. I bet she made some cinnamon rolls today. She told me she got a big tin of cinnamon the other day."

Lulu said, "She did, so let's git goin'."

That was the talk they had and nothing more needed to be said. One day Toady came home and told them all at the supper table that Mr. Burns had fixed up a spare room for her and asked her to move in with him and Irene so she could take care of her full time. Biddy started to say something and Lulu cut her short and said, "That there is gonna be a great thing for youense Toady. We is happy fer ya." And that was that.

CHAPTER 14

Abel Passes

The last time Abel came home it was to die. He was never sure what day his birthday was because his ma said it was October 29th one year and then she swore it was November 10th the next year. Each year it was always within the same two weeks, but for some reason the exact day was not clear. The year was not clear either and Abel told the kids he thought he was fifty when he came home. This time he had been gone a little more than a year and when he stepped up on the porch Rayleen screamed and told her sisters later, "He looked God awful pale, I thought he was ghost."

He did not look well. He was wearing raggedy clothes and his hair had not been cut for a while and was scraggly on his collar. His skin was looking thin as paper and he had broken his nose, which was already big and long and now it had a distinctive crook to it. He was hobbling and he was exhausted because he had walked a long way. How far, he would not say.

All of the kids took an interest in how poorly he was and Rayleen started feeding him and taking care of him in the daytime when everyone else was busy doing their own things. She put him in Mama's old bed, which had been occupied by Lulu and her, but she told her sister, "We gotta let him sleep there. He ain't long for this world, Lu."

Lulu agreed and even Biddy held her tongue when she saw him sitting all hunkered over in the rocker. They did try to get some information out of him, but he would not say where he had been or how things had become so bad for him health wise. Truth was, he did not want to talk about his gambling, the brutal beating he had taken as they threw him out of a moving truck somewhere north of Springfield. He did not want to share how he did not have food for a few days as he laid in a ditch thinking he was going to die from his injuries. No, he did not want to tell them any of that.

Arlan went over to Aunt Lutie's and then over to Uncle Elmer's and let them know that Pa was doing poorly and they did not know if they should call for a doctor or not. Aunt Lutie came over and she gave him some different teas to drink and checked out his body. She was the one who discovered that he had a couple broken ribs that were not healed and she bound his middle. She used muslin yardage and pinned it tight around his middle to ease some of that suffering. She also said, "Abel, you done broke yer nose! It's healed so I cain't reset it but damn, how did this all happen to ya?" Abel would not say.

She saw some bruising on his sides and on his back side and she quietly said to Lulu, "Somebody kicked the hell outta yer ol' man honey. I don't reckon he feels good about it, so jest don't go askin' about it."

Aunt Lutie determined a doctor would not help him and he had started to develop pneumonia. So she fixed hot mustard plasters and told the girls to keep him drinking water and tea all day. She would come over every few days and mix up more plaster and bring some chicken broth and help change his bedding because he had the sweats and would soak his night shirt and the sheets regularly.

Uncle Elmer and Aunt Bessie made sure that there was plenty of food and Uncle Elmer gave Lulu a nice sow who was close to farrowing and said, "Youense could use some hogs. Time to build up this here farm, Lulu."

Abel lasted about a month after he made it back. He did not suffer quite as much as Letty Anne had suffered, but there was suffering. Aunt Lutie did her best to keep him comfortable and she was able to teach Rayleen a lot of her home remedies. They kept a pot of water boiling on the stove with eucalypts leaves in it and camphor. It was good to have her there with her steady hand and her "take charge" attitude. The girls did whatever she needed them to do and she insisted on everyone keeping their tongue regarding Abel's past sins and focus on "gittin' him to the other side with Jesus".

When he died Uncle Elmer built the coffin, Rayleen and Lutie lined it and they buried him right next to Letty Anne. There was not so many tears falling during his service and fewer neighbors in attendance, but plenty of food was brought to the house and everyone was kind. The kids were quiet. They had so many mixed feelings about their Pa. Love mixed with resentment, sadness mixed with funny memories, and most of all, the feeling that their family had changed forever. They were officially orphans, as Rayleen stated over their first supper alone, when all the visitors and relatives had left.

Birdie cried quietly, with Willard holding her hand trying to comfort her. She still had that soft spot for Abel and she did not know why. Biddy saw it as a weakness. Lulu saw it as the mark of a good and kind heart. Birdie was always willing to turn the other cheek with everyone. She was a warm little woman with twinkling eyes and a ready laugh. Willard knew he had a gem in his Birdie and he kept his arm around her for the next fifty five years that they were married.

Changes

When the war was over and everyone who could come home had come home, there were a lot of changes that were inevitable. The small towns and the big towns all had suffered loss and the boys who came back to them were different. They wanted home and family and some good work. They had been to other countries, they had seen terrible things and listened to people speaking languages they could not interpret. They had been cold, hot, wet, wounded and hungry. They had seen darkness that was ink black and snow that was bloody. Things just were not going to be the same.

Everyone was happy to have Pod home. He came with a big smile, hugs all around, and said, "I am just fine, ever one, just fine. No need fer worryin'."

He stayed at his folk's place and Arlan came and sat with him or rode with him whenever he had a minute. He soon found out that Pod was not going to say anything about the war, but he did have some things to say.

It was a stormy day in October, low clouds and a stiff wind with the promise of rain coming. They were standing in the barn, looking at Orvil's latest purchase; two beautiful Percheron horses, geldings, black and shiny with thick black manes. He planned to work them some, but also to take them to county fairs and put them in team pulling contests. Orvil was deep into horse trading and was happiest when he was dickering with someone for a good price for stud services or a new colt or whatever it was. As long as it was horses, Orvil was happy.

Pod and Arlan were looking the two new arrivals over. Uncle Orvil had named them Baylor and Big Boy. They were gentle but huge and Pod was sitting on the stall gate, petting Big Boy. That is when he brought up the subject of Washington State. Arlan was all ears.

"Arlan, I met a man in the Army, Ralph Cotton, and he lives out there in Washington State in that there Yakima Valley. He told me they don't haul water ever and they never worry about drought. Guess they have what is called a canal system and water melts off them Cascade Mountains and they pull it right out of the rivers and put it in these long man-made rivers called canals and route it all over where farmin' is goin' on. He said people is plantin' trees like crazy, all kinds, and corn and beans and peas and wheat and all is growin' with what they refer to as irrigation. I mean to go see it."

Arlan smiled big and said, "Well then I aim to see it to. But I ain't comin' back once I get there."

Pod laughed and said, "Youense still wanna go, don't ya? Well, good, cuzzin I am goin'. I ain't got it all figured out yet, but I wanna go there and try that irrigation farmin'."

Arlan said, "You figure your pa and ma will go? I knowed no body over ta my place will leave Missouri."

Pod looked out the barn door and did not answer at first. Finally he sighed and said, "I got to git them to come. Ma cain't take losin' another one of her boys. I jest don't know how I am gonna get them to come. It'ld be better for Darla too. She and Jake could use a new place to grow they family. But nobody is gonna jump up and down and holler, yoohoo, I kin tell ya that."

Arlan nodded. "Yeah, ain't no body gonna jump up and down. Lulu knowed all along that I'm a goin', but she ain't said nothin' to the others. But you know, they all is happy with what they is doin' now. Biddy and Birdie are movin' to Kansas City real soon. Don't 'spect we will see too much of them after they get settled. Lulu and Rayleen and Ticky, they is gonna stick together forever, I 'spose. And you know, that Toady ain't leavin' the Burns place neither."

Pod said, "Yep. That there is the truth of the matter. You and me gotta figure out how we is gonna get my bunch to hop in a car and head west!"

That was the beginning of planning. It was 1945.

Part of the reason it would not be so hard to get Pod's family to consider the move was the fact that their part of the country had been experiencing a drought that had lasted about ten years. They had managed, with a well that did not completely dry up and good livestock, but the area was depressed and most people were just scraping by. Many people had started the migration when the Dust Bowl hit in 1935. Some of their good friends and some distant relatives had taken off for California and were writing home about good work, good weather, and water.

One of Uncle Orvil's cousins was in Fresno, working for the highway department and living in a little house on a tree lined street. His wife wrote often about the abundance of fruit and vegetables and the warm weather. She even sent a box of oranges for Christmas one year and another year some grapefruit, which were strange and tasted horrible to most of them. Darla took a liking to them and she got sores in her mouth from all the citric acid.

The cousins decided that Pod should write to Ralph Cotton and ask him about moving to Washington. Maybe he could tell them more about what to expect and how to navigate looking for work out there. They kept things to themselves for a while, thinking they would not put any pressure on Uncle Orvil and Aunt Lutie, since they were just glad the war was over and one of their boys was home. Some families were not as lucky. One neighbor lost all three boys and consequently, his wife, as she had a nervous breakdown and had to be put in the state run home up in Springfield. It was a rough time for many people.

The cousins heard back from Ralph. Pod read the letter to Arlan.

Dear Podrick,

I was really happy to get your letter. I am glad we are both home safe. The Yakima Valley is booming right now. There are lots of jobs and possibilities for getting started on a new life.

My Uncle Jim has a small house in Zillah, a small town not too far from where I live. He is planning to rent it out and if you could send some money, I think I can convince him to hold it.

How many of you are coming out? Once you get here, I have some people you can talk to about work.

Let me know if you are coming and if you are, send a money order for $25 made out to Jim Cotton and he will hold the house for you.

See you soon, I hope.

Sincerely,

Ralph P. Cotton

Arlan exclaimed, "Well he's a smart soundin' fella and it sounds like he is willin' to help us."

Pod nodded in agreement and said, "I think we need to sit down with the folks and Darla and Jake and talk about this here move."

The next day Pod went to Ava and got a money order for $25. Arlan gave him $12.50. The cousins continued to share all expenses in that way for years. Even when their wives did not understand it, they did and it was an unspoken pact between them. One for all, all for one, period.

The evening for talking it over was Saturday night that week in late April. Pod asked Darla and Jake to come over and asked his ma to make his pa's favorite supper, greasy greens, pinto beans, and fried spuds with cornbread on the side. He made sure Arlan was there and he told Arlan he would do the talking. It was spring and the door was open letting in a nice breeze. Aunt Lutie had set the table with a new cloth she had sewn from a blue gingham bolt she had bought from Lulu down at the store. Aunt Lutie had a set of matching dishes and she did not use them every day, but she must have felt like this was a special dinner because she used the good plates with blue blackberry vines around the edges and little farm scenes in the center. She put a blue pitcher of cold lemonade on the table too and Pod spied a lemon meringue pie on the counter.

Uncle Orvil and Aunt Lutie still said "grace" before dinner, but Arlan's family had dropped the habit when their ma died. But everyone bowed their heads at Aunt Lutie's and she always assigned "grace sayin'" to someone. Today she said, "Arlan, hows about you say the prayer for us."

Arlan hated it to be his turn, but he clasped his hands and shut his eyes, cleared his throat and said, "God bless us all. We is happy to be together. Amen."

Everyone murmured amen and the dishes started to round the table. At first there was just talk about the weather and the hogs and the horses. Jake and Darla talked about the little room they were renting from Willard Caster's parents. Pod and Arlan were quiet, mostly listening and then Pod cleared his throat and said, "Well, Arlan and I got somethin' we wanna talk to youense about."

Everyone stopped chewing and put their forks down. It just felt like one of those moments in life where you get a feeling things are going to change, right then, forever. He cleared his throat again and said, "Me and Arlan are gonna be headin' out to Washington State here in a few weeks. We got a house to rent and we is gonna get jobs workin' farms or somethin' when we get there. It's a perty place with lots of water and sun and you can see big mountains with snow on 'em right from the front porch."

Aunt Lutie looked at Pod and Arlan and burst out laughing. "You two, you think you is so smart and sneaky! Why, Orvil and I knew about what you was thinkin' for a long time now. You two are a pair to draw to!"

Pod and Arlan did not know what to say. Then Uncle Orvil chuckled and said, "I think you boys are perty damn smart, you know that? There ain't nothin' here anymore to keep ya. Why don't ya take Darla and Jake with ya?"

Pod started to open his mouth to speak and Darla jumped in first. "We was just waitin' for youense to invite us. I heard tell that the biggest fruit trees you could imagine grow out there. I wanna get me an apple tree and a pear tree and a peach tree. Right Jake?"

Jake shook his head yes. Jake was a quiet sort of fellow, but he was chuckling now too. "Youense got room for two more?"

Arlan looked at Pod, who was still speechless, and said, "Looks like we is goin' to Washington!"

Uncle Orvil put his hand up as if to stop conversation and said, "Me and Lutie, we is stayin' here. We like our place and I ain't movin' all my fine horses out there, but we will come and see youense once you get settled in. It ain't so far that we cain't drive there, I think."

Pod's eyes filled up with tears and he ducked his head to try and hide them. His shoulders shook and everyone just let him have a moment. Arlan said, "It would be nice to have you come Aunt and Unc, but I knowed it would be hard to walk away from this here place."

Aunt Lutie said, "Yes, it really would be hard for us. It ain't easy sayin' good-bye to youense either, but that Yakima Valley sounds like a good place to head to when you are settin' up a family boys. She sniffed and said, "I will miss you."

Arlan's sisters took it well. After all, they were all secure in what they were doing and none of them wanted to leave Missouri. They put together money and on Arlan's last night at the dinner table, Lulu stood up and gave a little speech as she handed over the cash.

"Arlan, we is proud of you. You have been a good brother to all of us. Sometimes we have felt like you was our Pa, seein' as how we got such a useless one and all. We knowed you will work hard and find a good life for yerself. Please accept our gift of $100 bucks to git ya started out there. We love you and you can always come home, anytime, no matter what. And, you can bring yer new wife yer gonna get from the beautiful Yakima Valley and bring her to meet your Missouri family. Amen."

The sisters clapped and cried and hugged Arlan until he thought he would burst. He even teared up but wiped them away quickly and stood to make his own speech.

"Thank ya all for the money. It is too much, but I 'precciate it 100%. I will write and keep ya informed of all my goings on out there. And likewise, you can come and see me anytime! Amen."

Rayleen made a blackberry cobbler for dessert and Biddy had churned some ice cream with the new ice cream maker she and Bill Butters bought to take to Kansas City. They sat around the table laughing and remembering all that they had been through and all that they hoped was in the future. They were a good family, born into poverty to two people who were like night and day, but were in love. The pain and the endless work that consumed their mama was not a distant memory for any of them. They kept it close and it drove them to work hard and to take care of each other. If Letty Anne could have seen them, she would have been bursting with pride. But they all believed she was there and little Ticky said, "We gots to say a prayer for Mama cuz' she is watchin' over us all." Lulu asked them to bow their heads and they all said a silent prayer to their dear mama, but poor old Abel, he did not get one, except for Birdie silently including him in hers.

CHAPTER 16

The Road Ahead

The drive west was a long one. It was not high summer, so the heat was not bad. Things were still green as they drove through valleys and mountains in the 1941 Chevrolet Sedan. Darla and Jake sat in the back seat with a big woven hamper between them. It had been loaded with ham sandwiches and biscuits and a pie, some bottles of water, and some cooked bacon wrapped in cheese cloth and a pot of boiled beans with a piece of salt pork cooked in them. They made it last for a long way.

Pod and Arlan took turns driving and kept the car gassed up. Jake was a bit of a mechanic and he would lift the hood regularly to make sure everything was connected and they had plenty of water and oil. Arlan was a fairly new driver. In fact, he was not licensed to drive, but that was never a concern where he came from. There were no state police in his county waiting to pull over the occasional car or truck lumbering down the dirt roads. There was no car in his name at home and no reason to have one. But Pod had given him driving lessons since he had returned from the war and Arlan had a fairly good idea of how to handle the car.

The top of the car was loaded down with 4 suitcases, one for each of them. The trunk was tied shut and had a box of tools for fixing the car and for the garage they all planned to have out west. It had some kitchen items so they could cook when they got there, some blankets, two double size bed rolls and a box with matches, bandages, a lantern, an ax, and coil of rope for any emergencies. There was a small camp stove and a folding card table too. Other than that, they left it all behind.

Pod could hear Darla weeping a few times as they drove along and he felt for her. He had cried on the train when he left Missouri for the army. He had felt so alone and he knew the chances of returning were stacked against him. But she had Jake, and he knew she could manage it. She was raised to work and to not complain. It was her job to help take care of her brothers and he knew she would do just that when they settled in. He snuck a glance at her in the mirror and he smiled at her pretty face with the brown hair cut in a bob. She looked like his Mama and Aunt Letty Anne. She was a slim girl and she was quiet like Letty Anne had been. He saw Jake take her hand and lean over and whisper to her. His only thoughts about Jake were that he had better not hit his sister.

Jake came from a family where their pa had whipped their mama on a regular basis. It was not because he was a drinker or because his wife was hard to handle. It was because his own pa hit his mama and he figured that was how you kept a wife. He whipped his boys now and then, but poor Mrs. Wright got the worst of it. She hid her bruises as best she could but Lutie sat behind her at church and saw the deep bruises on the backs of her arms and she knew when she missed church, she was probably nursing a black eye or worse, a tooth knocked out.

But no one interfered with those kinds of do-mestic problems back then. Those were things that happened and more often than a person might imagine. They were part of life for too many women and there was nowhere to turn. If you ran home to your mama, she might say, "Youense git on back home where you belong". Or worse yet, "What did youense do to make him hit ya like that?"

So, sometimes a sister or a daughter would bandage up the wounds or help with the cooking and cleaning when a woman got beaten so badly, she could not take care of the family. But mostly, these women just lived in a private hell of abuse and most often people turned their head the other way.

Lutie was hesitant about Jake and only because of the fact his pa beat on his ma. She talked to Darla about how that type of behavior is in the blood and like she said, "sometimes it jest comes to ya whether 'r not you want it." Darla just shook her head and declared that no one was as sweet and kind as her Jake. She was seventeen years old as they drove to Washington and she was sure she was driving to her best future.

Jake knew that Pod was watchful of him, but he had not felt like his pa and he just could not imagine himself ever hitting Darla. He had run away every time his mama had been hit, at least since he could run. His older brother, Leonard, had tried to take on the old man a time or two, but when the rage got in him, he was a monster. By the time Jake and Darla got married, all the kids but two young ones had fled home. None of them wanted to see their mama battered and bruised with her bones not set and the crooked way her right cheek bone had healed. No, Mrs. Wright would die not long after they left and every-one said at her grave, "She ain't gonna git hit no more now. God rest her soul."

At night they found places to camp along the way, by the roadside or in an actual campground. They took out the bed rolls and built small fires when they could and laid down to stare at the stars and dream about the life ahead of them. One night a farmer in Oregon walked down the road and asked them if they would like to bring their bed rolls to his grassy and shady front lawn. They were so grateful and his wife came out with a pitcher of cold lemonade and peanut butter cookies that were warm from the oven.

The farmer asked them about where they were headed and talked about his own journey to southern Oregon. He and his wife had come out in 1935 and settled into the Roseburg area. He said it was the best thing he ever did, leaving Arkansas. He now had 30 head of black angus cattle, 50 acres of farmland and a nice two story house, sitting in an oasis of big trees. The Umpqua River rolled by his property and he fished every Sunday in the summer.

He took the men out to his barns to see his livestock and his wife asked Darla if she would like to come inside. She even offered Darla a bath and Darla declined out of politeness, but she thought about that bathtub in the house all night. When they left in the morning, they were served up a wonderful breakfast with biscuits and gravy, sliced ham, fried eggs and a mountain of fried potatoes. Pod tried to pay them for the night's stay and they laughed and said, "Youense just be safe and get yerselves up to that Yakima Valley."

The night at the farmer's was their last night on the road. They drove all the next day up through Oregon and road on a little ferry that took them across the Columbia River. Before they got to the ferry they drove along the huge river and marveled at how wide and fast it was. They saw the famous Celilo Falls where the Indians fished on scaffolding that precariously hung out of over the great rocks of the falls. The river ran rapid and it was dangerous, but the salmon that were caught were part of the heart and soul of the tribes along the Columbia. The Missourians had never seen anything like the Indians fishing at the falls and they could hardly pull themselves a way. But they needed to get to the Yakima Valley.

Once they were on the Washington side, they started heading north up over the mountains on a winding road that took them past big evergreen trees where they saw deer standing in the tall grasses in the evening. They crossed what was called the Satus Pass and it was no more than a two lane road. They saw horses running across stretches of the road and Arlan said he thought they were wild horses. They even saw a bear sitting on a rock eating some kind of brush. They were in awe of it all.

It was about 4 a.m. when they drove over the mountains straight down into the wide Yakima Valley. The sun was just casting a soft yellow glow on the horizon as it climbed slowly up the distant hills. Pod pulled the car over and suggested they all get out for a stretch. Arlan was the first one to spot the snowcapped beauty of Mt. Adams. He let out a whoop and jumped up on the hood of the Chevy and said, "There it is! There it is! That there is Mt. Adams."

They stood at the side of road stretching and taking in the majesty of that beautiful mountain. The sun rose in the east and the mountain took on a soft pink glow where the bright white snow covered the peaks and valleys of the mountain sides. The air was cool and dry and they smelled a strong scent of some kind of vegetation and Pod walked over to inspect the field it came from. It was alfalfa, with a light dew on it and it glowed like a field of emeralds. He plucked a piece of it and inhaled the strong sent of the hay that it would become. Pod was teary eyed and he squatted down for a moment just to regain his composure.

Darla had picked a bouquet of wild sweet peas that were tangling up a fence that ran along the road. She was filling her arms with them and she was a sight to see with the billowy pink blossoms all around her young face. Jake leaned on the hood of the car and watched her and he felt a pang of jealousy and resentment inside. Sometimes when he looked at her, he felt that way. She was so good and so sweet and he knew she was a prize and something told him he was not good enough. But Darla had no idea that Jake felt that way. She would not even have been able to comprehend the twistedness of that.

Arlan was still admiring the view of Mt. Adams. He suggested they set up the camp stove and brew a little coffee and just enjoy it for a bit. Darla got out the small stove and sent Jake to get some water from the creek that was running under the bridge nearby. It was the Toppenish creek and it was clean and clear in those days. She brewed some coffee on the folding card table they had tied down in the back and the boys each took a cup and patted themselves on the back for being so smart to come out west.

They never forgot that cup of coffee or the smell of the alfalfa in the early morning or the clear skies that surrounded that beautiful mountain. Through all of their lives there were many changes, good and bad, but at that moment in time, everything was just as they wanted it to be. They were on the doorstep of a new life and damn, it was going to be good.

CHAPTER 17

Orchard Home

It was called a hired man's cabin and it was situated on the edge of a dirt road that led into the middle of an apple orchard. No one had lived there for a while, but Ralph Cotton and his wife, Muriel, had cleaned it to get it ready for the newcomers. When they pulled into the yard, Darla gasped because it had a grass lawn all the way around it and a big maple tree for shade. She could see a grape trellis running along the back yard and she thought maybe they were coming to the wrong house it was so lush. The house was painted white with red trim and it had a small screened in porch facing the back yard. It looked like a doll house to Darla.

But they were there and it was a welcome

sight to the weary travelers. The house had one bedroom, a small living room, a kitchen with room for a table and an indoor bathroom with a big tub and a sink. The only furniture was a table with mismatched chairs in the kitchen and an old chest of drawers in the bedroom. But there was an electric stove and refrigerator and running water all through the house. Ralph's wife had sewn some red checked curtains for the kitchen windows and hung some blue curtains in the bedroom.

The floors were a mix of linoleum and painted wood. The ceilings were low and when Ralph walked in to show them around, he had to duck at the front door. His wife Muriel was not with him on this first visit, but she sent over a box of fresh vegetables from the garden and a sliced ham.

Ralph was a tall drink of water and he had a shock of blonde hair that tended to stand up on his head when he ran his fingers through it, which was something he did often. He had a grin that was wide and big shiny white teeth. When he saw Pod the rest of them knew how close they had been in the war by the way he greeted him. He charged forward and grabbed his hand to shake it and then just pulled him into a giant bear hug and both of the men teared up and held onto that hug for a good long time.

Ralph shook hands with Arlan and Jake and he smiled that big grin at Darla and said, "Well, your brother wasn't kiddin' when he said you were a cute little gal!" Darla blushed and clasped her hands tightly together. She wanted to throw her arms around this big welcoming man and say, "I have never had an electric stove, or a refrigerator or an indoor toilet or a screened in porch or a grape vine or anything like this place!" Instead she nodded and said, "This looks like a very nice house Ralph."

Ralph grinned and said, "Well, it is on the small side, but it is a good price and it is real close to town and stores and all. You can find something bigger after you get settled in here."

Ralph carried the box of vegetables in the house and Pod followed carrying the ham in a big glass baking dish. Arlan trotted off down the road to see if he could get a glimpse of the mountain and Jake narrowed his eyes at Ralph wondering if he was that friendly to all of the women. He did not realize that Ralph was friendly to everyone. It did not matter who they were; he always stuck his hand out to shake it and once he knew you, he hugged hard and long.

When Ralph got ready to leave, he said he would be back in the morning to talk about some work possibilities. Before he drove away, he took Pod into the back yard and showed him a spigot for water. He said very seriously, "Pod, this is irrigation water. You cannot drink this water. This is just for watering the yard and the grapes and a garden if you get one going. Make sure no one drinks out of it or they are going to get really sick. It comes out of the canals and you cannot drink it."

Pod shook his head and said, "That there is somethin' I ain't never heard tell Ralph. Water that is just for the plants."

Ralph grinned and said, "You can drink the water that comes out of the kitchen and bathroom sinks though. That is well water and this place has a dandy well." He slapped Pod on the back and smiled big and said, "So glad to have you here Pod." Pod smiled and nodded his head. He had forgotten how demonstrative Ralph was and he knew it was something Arlan and Jake would have to get used to, but it was a good thing.

So they spent the first full night in Washington State on a little dirt road, in an orchard, on a rolling hill, smack in the middle of the Yakima Valley. As they fell asleep, each of them had a different dream in their head. Pod saw acres of land and a herd of cows and a truck to drive to town in. Arlan saw his own little house and it still was in an orchard and it still faced Mt. Adams but this time he added in a woman with dark hair. He knew she was there; he just did not know when he would meet her. Jake saw a shiny blue Buick sitting on a street in a small town and he was washing it with a hose and a bucket of soap.

Darla's dreams were right where she was and she imagined the house with some more furniture, flowers in the yard and a little bitty bassinette beside the bed with her sweet little baby that was already growing in her. She rolled over to tell Jake, but he was already asleep and so she simply ran her fingers through his hair and kissed his cheek and thought she had landed in heaven.

CHAPTER 18

Talkin' Funny

Arlan's first job in Washington State was picking cherries for an orchardist in the Zillah area. He had never seen a cherry tree or picked fruit for a living, but he watched the other pickers closely and started getting the hang of it that first morning. Strapping on his picker's bucket and climbing the ladders was the first thing to learn. Then how to pull the cherries with the stem and move quickly, just pulling the ripe ones, and making sure that you moved fast was the next thing to master.

He was in the orchard with all kinds of people. There were some fellows from Oklahoma and their whole family was with them. Women picked as well as men as children ran around under the big trees gorging on fallen cherries and throwing dirt clods at each other. There was one black family and they kept to themselves, but you could hear them singing a low song that set a rhythm to the picking. Arlan ate his lunch sitting on the edge of the bin, eating the ham and beans and a cold biscuit that Darla had packed for him.

It was in that orchard that he met another young man named Bryce Jones. Bryce was born and raised in the Valley and he was just fourteen years old, but he was a talker and he started asking questions about where Arlan came from right away. "You sound funny sir. Where did you come from?"

Arlan did not know if he liked being called funny, but he answered, "I come from Missouri, down in the south part of the state."

"Everybody talk like that were you come from?

"I reckon so."

"You ever picked cherries before?"

"No, cain't say that I have picked cherries."

"How do you like it?"

"Well, I knowed I ain't gonna do it fer too long."

Bryce started laughing and fell off the bin. "You really sound funny, Mr. Puckett. I have never heard anyone talk like you."

Arlan looked long and hard at Bryce and said, "Ain't yer ma and pa learned ya not to laugh at folks?"

At that Bryce straightened up and dusted off his work pants. They were not overalls like Arlan had on and he started to say something about that, but he got a look at Arlan's expression and thought better of it. "Excuse me Mr. Arlan Puckett. I forgot my manners there for a bit."

Arlan nodded and said, "I 'ppreciate that Mr. Bryce Jones." Then they both chuckled.

The cherry picking went on for a two week period and the days were long and they started at sunup, but about 2:00 they stopped for the day. It was the end of the first week when Bryce was picked up by his sister, Margaret. Margaret was nineteen and she was working waiting tables at the local café during the early morning shift. She pulled up to the grassy spot where the bin they had been filling was sitting. She was driving an old pick up and when she bounded out Arlan caught his breath.

Margaret had her hair cut in a bob and it was shiny black, almost blue. Her eyes were big and bright blue and her nose turned up a little on the end. Her sleeveless dress showed off her tan arms and the blueprint fabric matched her eyes. She still had on the apron from the café, tied tight around her waist and it was just the right touch to take his breath away. She saw her little brother dumping his last load of cherries in the bin and said, "Hurry it up Bryce. We have to pick up Mom from the warehouse."

Bryce looked over at Arlan and he got a devilish grin, seeing how Arlan could not take his eyes off of Margaret. Bryce said, "Hold up Maggie. I want you to meet someone. This is Arlan Puckett from Missouri. He's the one I told you talks so funny."

Margaret turned to face Arlan and gave him a dimpled smile. Arlan thought maybe she was laughing at him, the way Bryce tended to, but she said, "Nice to meet you Arlan. My brother is a pain. Get in the car now Bryce!"

As quick as she pulled in, she pulled the old pick up right over the orchard ruts and headed down the road with dust flying behind her. Arlan stared for a minute and thought, "I never even said howdy."

Pod had found work at a big dairy. He was gone by three in the morning and home by noon, smelling like cow manure and ready for food and a quick snooze. Darla set up a mattress on the back porch for him and it got the afternoon shade. She made sure he had a hot meal to eat and she washed his clothes for him in the wringer washer that was set up just off the kitchen. She strung a clothesline from the big maple to the side of the house and every day the clothes dried with the hot sun beating down on them.

Darla still had not told any of them about the baby. Jake had been a little anxious because he was the last one to find some work. But his job turned out to be the best one because it lasted all year long. He found work at a local garage that was looking for a mechanic to apprentice. It was exactly what he wanted to do. The pay was good and it would get better once he was fully trained. He talked about a house he was looking at in town that might come up for rent.

Darla was not sure she wanted to leave her brother and Arlan. They needed a woman around and if she told Jake they were going to have a baby he would try to get them into a house sooner. He did not like living with her brother and her cousin. He thought it was too cozy and that he could not have any priva-cy with his wife. He would complain to Darla whenever they were not around, but she just smiled and said, "We cain't afford to move out jest yet, Jake."

Darla was too busy to be lonely at first, and Ralph Cotton's wife, Muriel, started checking in on Darla a few times a week. She told her where to buy the cheapest groceries, where she could get a nice hair cut when she needed one, what her other neighbor's names were, etc. She was the first one to notice the bump under Darla's apron. Darla was mixing up a batch of biscuits for the noon meal and Muriel had just dropped by with some fresh carrots from her garden. Muriel had driven over in a car she drove everywhere. Darla was amazed that she could drive.

Darla offered her a cup of coffee in one of the four mugs she owned. Muriel sat down for "just a sec" as she stated and she looked at the slim young girl standing at the kitchen counter deftly mixing her dough.

"Oh Darla, I think I see a little bump under your apron. Is that what I think it is?"

Darla blushed and spun around to face Muriel and she started to cry right on the spot. "Oh Muriel, I ain't told a soul about this here baby. I jest am a little scared. I cain't talk to my mama or my cousins and I jest ain't sure what to tell the boys."

Muriel stepped over to the counter and slipped her arm around Darla and said "There, there honey. It is going to be all right. Having a baby is so natural and you are healthy and young. I can take you in to see the doctor, because that is what we do out here. Women don't have babies at home unless they are too far out to reach the hospital. So, you won't even have to worry about anything. There, there, the boys are going to be happy to think that a little one is coming."

Darla found herself resting her head on Muriel's shoulder wiping her tears with a flour covered hand. She did not know what to say about the doctor and a hospital. All she could think of was how would they ever afford all of that. But she stopped her tears and smiled and said, "I reckon I should tell 'em. Jake, he's been fussin' about movin' into town, but I cain't leave my brother and Arlan to fend for theyselves. I jest think tellin' him I'm expectin' will make him want to go right away."

Muriel said, "Well, it would be so nice for you and Jake to set up housekeeping by your-selves. After all, that is what young people do. They get a house and have a family and I am sure Pod and Arlan will both find someone to marry. You will see."

Darla smiled at Muriel and thanked her for her kindness. "Please don't mention the baby yet. I don't wanna spoilt the surprise for Jake."

After Muriel left Darla sat down at the small kitchen table and had another good cry. Things were different out here, she could see that clearly. Doctors for babies and you leave your kin, even if they need you, so you can have your own house and be separated and all. And women were driving cars. This was going to take some getting used to. She start-ed cleaning the carrots and wished she had some chickens to throw her scraps too. Then she thought that getting chickens was what she was going to do, before she told Jake. Who would want to leave chickens behind anyway?

CHAPTER 19

News from MO

The chicken pen went up and the garden spot was dug. There was not a lot to plant in June, but they decided to try some late beans and transplanted some tomatoes they got from a neighbor. Things were looking good.

Arlan brought home a couch that he got at a thing called a rummage sale in Toppenish, just over the river from where they lived. He also bought a floor lamp and a box of dishes which included some glasses and silverware.

Muriel took Darla to "town" in Toppenish and she bought some yardage from the J.C. Penney store and made curtains for the living room and a new dress for herself with a bigger waistline. Then she decided to tell Jake about the baby.

They were snuggled into bed and Jake had just brought home a screen to put in the window of their bedroom. They could smell the grass that Ralph had come by and cut for them that afternoon. Darla had treated her flock to some grass cuttings. The air was cool, as it often was in the evening, because the Yakima Valley was really a desert. Without irrigation it was dry and covered in sage brush, but the water had changed all of that.

Darla said to Jake, "I wanna tell ya Jake, we is havin' a little one." Jake rolled over and looked at his beautiful little wife laying there in the summer twilight and he almost hollered but remembered the other men of the house sleeping on the porch.

"That is just the best thing ever, Darla. Just the best thing. A little boy, namin' him Thomas, I swear, a little boy for us."

Darla giggled softly and said, "What ifen it's a girl?"

Jake scoffed and said, "Then youense can name her. It don't matter none anyway. We is havin' a baby!"

The next morning was Sunday and everyone was home for an early breakfast. They had not found a church they wanted to attend just yet, so big breakfasts became the new way to give thanks. They had some money and could buy meat from a grocery store, so there was always bacon, ham or sausage. The plans they had for raising some hogs were for the next year when Pod hoped to buy a place of his own. So there was ham and eggs, fried potatoes, biscuits, and cherry jam that Darla had made the first week she could get some jars and a canning kettle.

Darla informed her brother and cousin about the baby and it was a big celebration around the table. Arlan said, "That'll be the first little Washington baby borned into the family!" Right then Darla knew if she had a girl she would call her Rose after the wild roses that grew in the ditch out front and made the yard smell like heaven.

That first summer was good for the Missourians. They ate well, they had work, Darla's pregnancy was going well and the little house in the orchard became a home. They reveled in the fruits and vegetables that were everywhere. Darla canned peaches and pears and made applesauce and apricot jam from the big tree in Muriel and Ralph's yard. They dug a cellar and put in spuds and onions. Everything they grew or got from someone else was big, ripe and delicious. It was a bounty and they wrote home to tell the folks about it. Arlan was sure someone else would move out once they heard about how plentiful good food and work was in Washington.

But the Missourians at home were happy

enough and they did not plan to move west. Especially Aunt Lutie. She was getting sick that summer, slow and steady, much like her sister Letty Anne. She could not eat much and her energy was disappearing. Uncle Orvil called on the nieces, Lulu and Rayleen, to come over and help tend to her. Lulu insisted that a doctor be brought in and Uncle Orvil took his '44 Ford over to fetch the new doctor as Doctor Thomas had died when his pickup truck got hit by train. The new Doctor was named Fredericks and he was from Virginia. He was as country as they were and everyone agreed he fit in nicely there in southern Missouri, on the edge of the Ozarks, just north of Arkansas.

He diagnosed Lutie Taylor with the same diagnosis as her sister Letty Anne. It was a blow to them all and they knew just how hard her death would be. The discussion was what to tell the folks who had gone to Washington. They worried for Darla with the pregnancy and they knew how hard Pod and Arlan were going to take losing Lutie, but the decision was made, mostly by Lulu, that they needed to be told. Lulu wrote the letter that they sent.

Dear Pod, Arlan, Jake and Darla,

We was so glad to get your letter telling us about the baby. It sounds like youense are eating well and working hard. Darla, you be sure to rest between batches of canning. You don't want your feet to swell like Mama's did.

We have some news that we hate to give you. There ain't no easy way to say it. Lutie is feeling very poorly. The new doc told us she is dying of the same thing that our Mama died from. It is the cancer in her stomach. I am so sorry we have to tell you this way but we ain't got a phone number to call youense at, so we just have to send this here bad news in a letter.

Rayleen, Ticky and I are taking turns caring for Lutie. She is quiet and takes the medicine the doctor gives her to fight off the pain. Pod and Darla, your Pa is pretty shook up, but he says for youense to stay put and make your lives in the west. Once Lutie passes, he wants we three girls to leave our place and move in with him as you know, he has the better house and land. As much as we hate to leave where Mama lived, we think it will be best for your Pa and it's still close to my job.

Please keep sending us letters and we will keep sending letters to you. If youense can find a phone we can call we will be glad for that. That way, as things go a long we can keep you in the know. You don't need to come home. Like as not, you wouldn't make it here before she passes on.

Love to all of ya,

Lulu

Darla got the letter out of the mailbox and she was the first to open it. When Pod came home in the afternoon, he found her sitting in a kitchen chair staring at the wall. Her tears were dried but her hand was shaking when she handed him the letter. He plopped down beside her and put his head in his hands once he read it. Their hearts were broken. They could not speak for quite a while and when they did Pod said, "This here is gonna be hard on us, but we knew when we left home we was leavin' ever'thin' behind us. We just cain't let it keep us from settlin' in here."

Darla looked at Pod and she said, "I want to go home and live in Missouri, Pod. I miss Mama and Pa and I miss people that talk like us and I don't care how much fruit there is and water and all, I jest want my family."

Pod hugged her and said, "Darla honey, you is home. This is where you belong. You is gonna make a family here and so am I and so is Arlan and this is our new place. We ain't goin' back, no how, and that is all there is to it. Mama would be so sad ifen you went back. She wants this for youense."

Darla walked into the small bedroom and laid down on her bed and cried until it was time to fix the men some supper. She cried every day for weeks, but she kept going forward, just the way Pod wanted her to and the way her mama had taught her.

Arlan and Jake took it hard, especially Arlan. Aunt Lutie had been his favorite relative since he could walk over to her place when he was a little boy. He thought about her fried apple pies sitting on the counter and her big sunflowers growing in the garden and the way she always made sure he had a place at her table any time, any day. He thought about how she had taken such good care of Mama and Pa when they died and he was glad that Lulu and Rayleen could take care of her. He thought about Uncle Orvil and how sad he must be, looking out from his porch, wondering what he will do without Lutie.

Pod arranged for them to use Ralph Cotton's phone number and sent it back to Lulu. He and Darla wrote a letter for their Ma and Pa. Arlan wrote a letter to his sisters. Jake was quiet and he worried about his little bride and the baby being affected by such sadness. But everyone got on with it. They got on with working.

Arlan got a job on a big ranch in Toppenish and bought himself an old pick up. He worked with the cattle and horses and built fences and repaired whatever needed fixing. He stayed in a little cabin on the ranch during the week and came back to stay with the family on Sundays. He just kept his head down and worked hard and let his sorrow rest in his chest.

It was during this time that he happened on to Margaret Jones again. He was headed home on a Saturday afternoon and he decided he would stop and buy some groceries for the family. He pulled up to the small grocery store in Zillah. It was part of the main street and it was located on the ground floor of a two story building. It had a big screen door on it and the wood floors were splintered and dark with wear. He was getting used to the stores and he liked to buy a little sweet for Darla as she had been craving sweets since she got pregnant. He was standing looking at all the candy when someone stepped beside him. When he looked up it was Margaret Jones, Bryce's sister. She had a red bandana tied on her hair and her thick black bangs curled up on her forehead. She said, "Hello there Mr. Puckett."

Arlan nodded politely and said, "Hello there Miss Jones. You can call me Arlan ifens you like."

Margaret grinned and said, "Okay, Arlan. I have never heard that name before. Are you named after your father?"

"No, my father was named Abel. I reckon I don't know who I is named after, but I am the only Arlan I know."

Margaret picked up a Milky Way candy bar and said, "This is what I came in here for. I like to put it in the freezer and eat it when it's good and frozen. You should try it."

She was gone as quick as she appeared and it left Arlan a little flustered. He wanted to say something more, but he did not know what to say. He wanted to ask her if he could come by and see her, but he just was not sure if that was the right thing to do. He did not know if she could ride in a car with him or if her folks wanted her to be chaperoned. He just felt like there was too much he did not know, so he watched her saunter out of the store. Right before she let the screen door thwack shut, she turned and gave him a big grin and a little wave and he could not tell if she was teasing him or flirting or what she was doing. He just smiled back, awkwardly, and he knew his cheeks turned red.

Arlan had not really made any friends yet. He was shy and he knew he stood out because of his size, but he was too shy to make friends. His black hair and his big and tall frame made people look twice at him, but he was not sure if they were laughing at him or just wondering who he was. He felt out of his element and he wanted to fit in.

When he got to the house, he decided to try to talk to Pod about it. He had noticed Pod was pretty at ease around everyone and he figured it was because he had been in the service and had gone to other places and met a lot of people who were not from Missouri. He even thought Pod was possibly dating someone. He was not there during the week, but he had heard Darla say that Pod had come home, taken a bath, dressed in his best clothes and left before supper one night. She said Pod would not say what he was doing, but Jake and Darla thought it must be that he was courting someone.

Pod gave him some advice. He said, "Arlan, youense have got to get some confident ways about ya. Out west, these girls are used to drivin' and workin' outside of they homes and they are more forward than girls back home. Ifens you want to date one of them, you jest go up to her and say, 'how would you like to go for a drive and get a soda pop?' and then just take her over to Toppenish and pull into a drive up restaurant and get her a soda. It's easy Arlan. Jest do it."

Arlan said, "Do I have to ask her Pa or Ma?"

Pod said, "No. It don't work like that out here. She kin decide if she wants to go with ya' er not. You just have to get to askin' her."

Arlan was uncomfortable with this information. He was used to independent women because his sisters were pretty independent.

But he was not used to dealing with parents of young ladies and he did not want to make a fool of himself. But he thought about it for a few weeks and again, he saw Margaret, but this time he was getting gas at the filling station where Jake worked as a mechanic. He had pulled forward from the pumps and had gone back to say "howdy" to Jake when he looked up and saw Margaret Jones pull up in the old pickup truck he had seen her drive in the orchard. She stuck her head out the window and said, "Hello there Arlan."

Arlan strolled over to her window and said, "Hello there Margaret." She grinned and hopped out of the truck and said to the attendant, "Timmy, I need you to fill it up and put it on my Dad's tab. Thanks." She walked over to Arlan's truck and said, "This is a nice rig you bought. How do you like it?"

Arlan cleared his throat and said, "I like it fine. It's my first ever vehicle."

Margaret grinned her dimpled grin and said, "You are a funny one Arlan Puckett. When are you going to ask me out on a date?"

Arlan looked at her and stammered, "Right now, I guess. You wanna ride with me to get a soda pop?"

Margaret giggled and said, "Sure Arlan. I will ride with you to get a "soda pop". Just follow me home and I will hop in with you."

Arlan and Margaret started going to get a soda pop on a regular basis. Margaret informed him that they just called it pop in Washington. Then one day Margaret said, let's go eat a meal now, and before you knew it, Arlan was dating that pretty little black haired girl who could drive a pickup truck, wait tables in the café, and keep him smiling all day.

CHAPTER 20

Podrick Randall

The fall of the year came and with it came more changes for the Missourians in Washington. Jake did get a house in town for him and Darla. She was very reluctant to leave her brother, but the new little house had a nursery for the baby and it had a big garden and a fenced in yard. It was freshly painted inside and out and Jake bought her a crib and a new sewing machine.

The baby was not due to be born until January, so there was plenty of time to settle in. Darla met some neighbors and she started to feel less lonely. Muriel took her to Toppenish to see a doctor and he told her that she would do just fine with her birth. He said she could even try having it at home if she wanted, but Muriel objected and told her she would talk with Jake and help him to understand that the baby would need to be born in a hospital.

Darla got letters from home and was lonely for her cousins and wished she was taking care of her mama. But she knew she could not go home to help, so she just got busy making baby clothes and baby quilts and fixing up her new little home.

Jake was happy there and he felt very proud of his job and the fact he could get a house before her brothers. In fact, he was rather boastful about it and it embarrassed Darla more than a little. She knew that her brothers were hard working men and that they would have homes and furthermore they would have land, but she could not get Jake to tone it down. He was on the arrogant side and when he came home with a brand new car, she broke down in tears. "How can we afford it? We have to pay for the baby Jake. That hospital ain't free."

Jake just laughed at her and said, "Stop cryin'. Youense ain't in Missouri no more. I got insurance at my job for the hospital and this here car gets paid in payments, not all at once. We pay the bank $35 a month and it's ours. You got to trust me, damnit. I ain't a stupid hillbilly, like yer brother."

This made Darla cry harder and that made

Jake madder. He grabbed her wrist and twisted it hard and pulled her up into his face. "Look here little Miss. You stop that now. I ain't gonna listen to you cryin' about us havin' what we need. You wipe that face and get out in that car and we is goin' for a ride."

That was the first time Jake touched her and it hurt. But it would not be the last time.

It was October when Ralph pulled up to the little house in the orchard and told Pod that the family from Missouri had called and they wanted him to call as soon as he could. He went over to Ralph's place and made the long distance call to the store in Noble. Lulu answered and he knew by the sound of her voice his Mama was gone. She told him that she passed peacefully and that they were planning to bury her right next to her sister Letty Anne. She told him that she said she loved them before she died and not to feel badly because they were in Washington. But Pod did feel bad and so did Arlan and Darla when he told them. When he left Ralph's he pulled out $10 to pay the long distance and even though Ralph refused it, he stuck it under the phone anyway and walked solemnly to the car so he could go and tell his sister and cousin.

On the day of Lutie's funeral, Darla fixed a dinner for her brother and cousin and they invited Ralph and Muriel to come and Arlan invited Margaret. They fixed Lutie's favorite dinner: fried potatoes, green beans cooked slow in a hunk of salt pork, cornbread, and apples fried in bacon grease. They had a peach pie for dessert and Muriel brought homemade vanilla ice cream. They sat around the dining room table that Jake had purchased and it came with eight chairs, so they even had a spot for one more. Just as they got ready to sit down, there was a knock at the door and Pod jumped up and answered it. Standing there was a beautiful woman with bright red hair and bright red lipstick. Pod hugged her and said, "Ever body, this is Carol. I invited her to eat with us."

Darla jumped up to get another plate and Muriel exclaimed, "Hello Carol! I didn't know that you and Podrick were friends." Then she turned to the rest of them and said, "Carol went to school with me."

Darla could not take her eyes off of Carol's red hair and Jake was staring at her large breasts under her tight white sweater. Arlan was speechless and Margaret squeezed his leg and giggled. Pod sat her down right beside him and grinned from ear to ear.

Carol said, "Hello everyone. I am sure you were not aware that Pod or as I like to call him, Randall, and I are seeing each other. But here I am!"

Carol had a way of talking that brought all

eyes on her, with the red hair, the red lips and the way her hands moved all around when she talked. She boldly leaned over to Pod, or Randall, and gave him a peck on the cheek. Randall blushed but you could see he was smitten with Miss Carol Simpson. Randall put his arm around her and said, "I reckon you can all call me Randall now. Pod is a little bit hillbilly, as Carol says."

Arlan narrowed his eyes a little and would have liked to say something, but Margaret squeezed his hand and smiled brightly into his face. She knew Arlan was sensitive, especially about the word "hillbilly" and "Okie", which were used freely in the Yakima Valley at the time to describe anyone who was not born and raised there and had any kind of accent. But like she had said to him, "Arlan, if you want to talk differently, then do it. If you want to talk like you are from Missouri, then do it. Either way, I don't mind because I just love you for who you are." And that was the way Margaret was about Arlan. She blessed the day he moved to Washington and she thought he was the finest man she knew or had ever known. When her father asked her what Arlan's people were like, she said, "Like they are from Missouri, Daddy. They talk different, eat different, they even treat family different. But I plan to marry him and you can just get used to it."

Mr. Jones chuckled and said, "That a girl, Margaret. Mother, I do believe that girl has always had a mind of her own." Her mother just smiled and nodded her head. There was nothing she had ever been able to tell Margaret that Margaret did not already have an opinion about and the ability to tell you why. Why would finding a husband be any different.

Jake was also offended, but he had already told Darla that she was acting like a hillbilly on more than one occasion. He was always trying to get her to stop running food out to her brother and to stop crying over Missouri and to just stop being Darla. He was slowly but surely pushing her down and her brother could see it and Arlan could see it, but Darla was only focused on having the baby, so they just kept it to themselves.

Muriel kept a close eye on Darla. She had pulled into Darla and Jake's one day shortly after Carol had told them to call Pod Randall. She was delivering some pears she had just picked and was surprised to see that Jake was home. She thought he must have come home for lunch and maybe was taking a longer break. As she walked toward the backdoor, she heard a door slam and she heard Jake say, "Get your ass out here Darla Ray. I told you no more takin' beans and cornbread out ta Pod's or Randall's or whatever. He can fend for hisself!"

She heard a whimper out of Darla so she shouted "Hello! Hello! It's Muriel. I brought some pears for you." The screen on the back-door swung open and Jake stepped out with his greasy hair hanging in his eyes and as he pushed it off his forehead he said, "Howdy Muriel. Darla will be out in a minute. I am headed back to work."

He brushed by Muriel on the sidewalk and revved up the engine on his car and sped out of the driveway. Muriel stood still and waited for Darla to come out on her own, but she did not. So Muriel walked up to the door and looked in the screen. Darla was sitting at the table with her head in her hands silently crying. Muriel put the box of pears on the porch and walked on into the kitchen and sat down beside her. "Honey, are you all right?"

Darla lifted her head up and Muriel saw the red mark on her cheek. It was fresh and it had a little split in it. It was beginning to swell and Muriel could see that it would turn purple, but not too purple. It was a quick punch he must have laid on her, not a hard one with full force. Muriel reached for her and Darla shook her head no and said, "Ya cain't say nothin' to Pod. Ya jest cain't. He will beat the livin' hell outta Jake. He has warned him afore."

Muriel went to the sink and got a dish cloth and ran cool water on it. She noticed the pot of beans on the stove and a pan of cornbread beside them. She handed the cool cloth to Darla and said, "I can deliver these beans and cornbread to your brother on my way home. You do not need to worry about anything honey."

Darla started to cry again and as she cried, she rocked back and forth, holding her belly. "Jake's Pa was mean. He beat his Ma regular. I jest thought Jake was different. I jest thought he was no way gonna hurt me." She shook her head back and forth and said, "I jest gotta hang on for this here baby. He might not hit me once I is holdin' a baby."

Muriel sat down in a chair and looked at Darla. She was such a pretty little woman. She was thin and her hair was thick and it was cut right at her chin. Her eyes were beautiful and they changed from blue to green depending on what she wore. Today they were green and her little hands were trembling as she wiped away the tears. Muriel did not know just what to do. She thought Randall should know and she thought Arlan and Ralph should know too. She thought they could put pressure on him and make him stop. But she knew that Darla was right; it would probably mean that they made Jake leave Darla or worse yet, what if he took Darla away or what if he really beat her when he found out they knew. He would blame Darla for sure. Muriel needed to think.

So, she picked up the bean pot and carried it out to the car and came back and got the cornbread. She grabbed a jar of fresh apple sauce from the counter and took that too. She kissed Darla on the top of the head and said, "Any time, day or night, you call me or come to me or whatever it takes, but you do not have to let that man hit you. It is wrong and you just don't have to live that way out here."

As she drove away, she was so angry with Jake that she wanted to stop and tell him so and she wanted to tell his boss too. But she knew she needed a better plan than that, because after all, that would just get Darla beaten up.

When she pulled into the shade of the big maple in Randall's yard, he stepped off the porch to greet her. She smiled and waved and said, "Your sweet sister sent you some beans."

Randall smiled and opened the door for Muriel. She was always so touched by his po-lite and gentle ways, the same way that Arlan acted. But they were not kin to Jake and it showed. She held her tongue this time, but as she drove away, she knew she could not keep this secret for long.

CHAPTER 21

Inheritance

Lulu, Rayleen, and Ticky had packed up their house and moved over with Uncle Orvil. The house they lived in had been rented all these years from a Mr. Carter, but he lived up in Springfield, so they just sent a letter to let him know they were leaving.

Uncle Orvil's house was bigger than their old one and he had three bedrooms, a living room, a kitchen, a big front porch, a two seater out house, a nice barn with corrals and a good chicken pen. He had his horses and his wagons and he had been able to save enough money in the bank that he did not have to have any enterprise going now that made money. He did send his studs out for service and he sold some hogs occasionally. He told the girls if they wanted to bring the chickens over, he was fine with them continuing to sell eggs.

Lulu sat down with him before they moved in to talk about the arrangement they would have once they were established at his house. She was a businesswoman at heart and she had thought ahead to what kinds of things they needed to settle on to keep things peaceful. First, she wanted to pay rent to Uncle Orvil. She had been paying Mr. Carter since her Ma died and she figured it was a fair price. Uncle Orvil said no, he would not take it, but if she insisted, he would put it in a savings account for them. Lulu said she was paying it to him and she did not expect to get it back.

They agreed that Rayleen would do the cooking and gardening, Ticky would take care of the animals and especially the chickens but Uncle Orvil would need to teach her to care for the horses. They had a hog over at their old place that Uncle Elmer had given them, but he had long ago been butchered. But Ticky said she knew about hogs because Uncle Elmer had taught her how to care for them.

Lulu was still working for Mr. Burns at the General Store and she would continue to do that, but Uncle Orvil wanted to teach her to drive his 1939 Ford so she did not have to walk every day. The move to Uncle Orvil's put them about five miles farther from Noble and he just did not think a woman her age should be walking seven or eight miles a day to get to work and that was only one way. Lulu reluctantly agreed but insisted she would pay for the gasoline.

For food they would use the garden and split the cost of things they got from the General Store. Uncle Orvil would always ask how much he owed her and Lulu would always say $2.00 and Uncle Orvil would always say, "Na, it cain't be that, Lulu. Youense is payin' too much." But Lulu insisted and he was too old to argue. He just was so happy that he had someone to live with him. He missed his Lutie so much but having her nieces there really eased the blow. He would never have wanted Podrick and Darla to return on account of him. He just could not bear the thought of taking their dream away from them.

Rayleen had been in Aunt Lutie's kitchen many times and she knew just where everything was located. She moved a few things in, especially her favorite skillet and her best biscuit pan. She rearranged the dish cupboard and added in some of their favorite bowls and plates. Aunt Lutie had a matching set of dishes that Uncle Orvil had bought her when they celebrated their twenty fifth wedding anniversary. They were white with blue blackberry vines around the edges and a picture of farmstead in the center. Lutie had been so proud of them that she had built herself a special shelf to keep them on. Rayleen dusted it and left things exactly as Lutie had placed them. They used those dishes every Sunday after church and Ticky lovingly dried them and put them away.

Sometimes on a Sunday Toady would come out after church and have Sunday dinner with them. The four sisters enjoyed those afternoons, swapping stories, rereading letters from the family in Washington, eating good food and laughing about their childhood.

Toady had a new hairdo these days. It was cut and permed and it made her even prettier. She had started dressing differently and she always had on earrings. The sisters thought it was silly, but Toady seemed happy, enough, but never full of the joy she used to radiate. Her life was strange and so much of it did not see the light of day. She now slept in Irene's room with her. Mr. Burns had another room in the house. He was still a good and calm man and between Toady and Ruby Porter he was well cared for. It was just a different sort of family and no one really knew what to call it, so people just said things like, "over at the Burn's place" and rolled their eyes or smirked.

It was on one of these Sundays that they got word that Darla had given birth to a baby girl,

Rose Ray Wright. They heard she was a small baby at six pounds 5 ounces, but that she had a head full of brown hair and big blue eyes. They ooo'd and aaah'd and wished they could hold her. She was the first baby in their family since Ticky was born.

It was in the spring that year that Jake got a notion in his head about the arrangement in Missouri with Uncle Orvil and the cousins. It was a Saturday afternoon and baby Rose was napping and Darla was mending some pants, when Jake said, "I've been a thinkin' 'bout yer Pa's place. What happens when he dies, to the place I mean?"

Darla looked up and thought for a minute and said, "I don't know Jake. I imagine it goes to me and Randall. I reckon that'll happen."

"Well, I wouldn't be too damn sure 'bout that Darla. Now that them three girls is livin' there, they might just think they are gonna git that farm. I mean, why not? Your Pa lettin' them stay there for free and all."

Darla shook her head and said, "Pa cain't make it without my cousins. He is lucky they are there and anyways, we cain't go back and stay there, now can we? You said I had to forget about home and all."

Jake stretched his legs out and looked hard at the ceiling and said, "Have you asked Pod what he thinks?" Jake refused to call Pod by his new name, Randall, but Darla did because she respected her brother and if he wanted it, then that is what she would do. But she did not ask Jake to stop calling him Pod. She did not need Jake to get angry.

Just then they heard the crunch of tires in the driveway and Jake jumped up to look out the window. "Ahh, looks like Pod hisself jest pulled up."

Randall did not knock when he entered in the house. That was a custom that he and the Missouri group just could not get used to. They did not knock much at home. It was usually kin folk coming to see you or the screen was open wide or you just hollered that you were there. Either way, Randall did not take up knocking when it came to family.

"Hello there sis. Where's my little Rosie?"

"She's sleepin' Randall. How's you doing?"

"Jest fine. I am due over to Ralph's d'rectly, but I just wanted to stop in and see how my little niece is gettin' on."

Jake said to Darla, "Ain't there somethin' youense want to ask Pod, Darla?"

Randall glared at Jake, but he then turned to Darla and said, "What is it sweetheart?"

Darla started to open her mouth but Jake jumped in first and said, "Is you and Darla gonna git yer Pa's place when he kicks the bucket?"

Randall frowned and said, "Well, I reckon so Jake. What in the hell do ya wanna know that fer?"

"You knowed that them three cousins of yourense are livin' there with your Pa now and I jest got to thinkin', they might think that place is theirs on account yer Pa is lettin' them live there for free and all."

Randall looked at Darla and she put her eyes down toward her mending, but not before he saw the look of disgust on her face. He turned to Jake and said, "What makes youense think that they is livin' there for free?"

Jake said, "Well, I jest figure yer Pa, seeing as how he likes them so much, maybe he jest ain't plannin' to make them pay. Ya know he's got a soft spot for them girls. And them bein' women on their own and all..."

Randall chuckled and said, "Youense don't know nothin' 'bout my girl cousins. They ain't the kind who depend on men. I reckon they take care of themselves and Pa jest fine."

Jake stood up then and said rather abruptly, "Well, I didn't figure you for someone who would let his sister and her baby get screwed outta of they's inheritance!"

Randall was a calm man, very steady. No one had seen him get fired up before he went off to war or now that he was back. In fact, he prided himself in being respectful and polite to everyone. But he never did like Jake. He just never had trusted him, no matter how many times Darla said she was doing fine being married to him. He always felt like Jake was coiled up inside like a snake and he would strike any minute. Randall looked at Jake now and said in a deep and quiet voice, "Never you mind what Darla and Rose's inheritance is gonna be. You ain't got no stake in it."

Jake stepped closer to Randall and said, "Like it or not, Podrick Randall, I am her husband and I git half of anythin' she gits, so I gotta a stake in it all right."

Randall stepped closer to Jake now and he said, "Like I said Jake, it ain't none of yer concern and ya better remember that." Then he spun around and left the house as quick as he came.

Darla started to cry and Jake turned and looked at her with loathing. He stepped toward her and reached out and slapped her face. Then he grabbed her hair and said, "Ifen you git one dime, I'm gonna take it Missy. Yer big strong ass hole of a brother cain't stop me." Then he pushed her hard and she fell off the chair and Jake walked out the back door and left.

Darla got treated like this most of the time. Sometimes he might go for a week or two without striking her, but that was as long as that lasted. He liked to keep her scared and he used all different methods of abusing her, careful to not leave marks if he could. He knew where to punch and where to kick and Darla could not duck fast enough.

Muriel had stayed quiet about the day she saw the bruise, but she saw how Darla reacted when she saw him coming home. She would never leave the house without his permission and she always was quieter when he was around. Muriel checked on the baby too, because she was afraid, he might hit the little one. But so far, no sign of that.

A few days after the inheritance talk, Muriel got a call from the pay phone downtown. It was Darla and she was asking if Muriel would come by and pick her up. Muriel said she would but it would be an hour or two before she could get there. Darla said, "Muriel, please come right away."

Muriel dropped her rolling pin on the counter and turned off the bubbling cherries on the stove and threw off her apron. She was in the car and pulling out of the driveway before she realized her oven was on. But that would have to wait. Darla needed her and that meant it was urgent.

She pulled into the driveway at Darla's and jumped out of the car as she turned it off. The backdoor was open and the first thing she saw was an old suitcase with a baby blanket folded over it. She hollered for Darla and she came down the hallway, holding baby Rose in her arms. Her lip was bloody and her left eye was swollen shut. There were bruises on her arm that were in the shape of fingers and her hands were shaking.

Muriel picked up the suitcase and motioned for the car and within two minutes she had whisked the two little women out of the house. There was no talking for the first ten minutes and when Muriel pulled into her driveway, she turned and looked at Darla for the first time and she said, "You are not going back to that house. We are going to figure this out. When Ralph gets home, he will go and get your brother and some decisions can be made. Do you hear me, Darla?"

Darla turned and looked out the window and said, "I dunno what I is s'pposed to do. I jest dunno."

CHAPTER 22

Couples

Margaret and Arlan were a couple now. They saw each other every day and they were simply crazy about each other. Margaret liked it when Arlan called her Maggie, so her whole family started calling her that. She brought Arlan over to her parent's house for dinner so often that Arlan told her mother, "I hope youense don't think I is spongin' off of ya. I would be glad to pay for my food, ifen you need me to."

Mrs. Jones laughed and said, "No thank you Arlan. We love having you here. You are just like family to us, so do not worry about the food!"

Arlan liked the way Maggie's family ate. It was different than his family. They rarely ate things awash with bacon grease. The only time he saw it used was for frying eggs for breakfast. Sometimes they had breakfast at night and he was introduced to waffles, which he had a great liking for. Her mother put bowls of fresh vegetables on the table and half the time they were raw, especially when the garden was producing. They ate some meat, but it was not the highlight of every meal and her mother made light and delicious homemade breads and rolls. Her soups and stew were not like his families, which consisted of whatever was left over and just put in the pot with beef or chicken broth. She only had a few ingredients in them and everything was fresh and flavorful.

They had never had biscuits and gravy though, so he asked Darla if she would make them some and bring them over. Mrs. Wright insisted Darla come to her kitchen and make them there and eat breakfast with them. The Sunday Darla came was a few days before the day she left Jake.

Darla arrived with Jake at about 8:00 a.m. on a Sunday. The Wright's lived in a big two story white house, that sat on a hill of trees with a big green lawn. They had a huge garden and a fenced off pasture for their Hereford bull and their few cows. It was an oasis in the hot valley.

Darla was shy, but she loved Maggie, so she stepped right into the kitchen with Mrs. Wright and Maggie and put on the apron she had brought along. Mrs. Wright's name was Velma and she insisted that Darla call her by her first name. Darla usually said, "Mrs. Velma" when she spoke to her as she felt such respect for her.

Velma's kitchen was all red and white checks. The gingham curtains, the lineoleum, the tablecloth, even the cannisters on the counter were red and white checks. She had a big country sink that was about five feet long with a built in porcelain drain board. Her flour bin drawer was located right by the longest counter. Darla decided she would like to have one of those too.

Velma asked her to sit down for a cup of coffee first and Velma bounced little Rose on her knee. Darla thought how her mother would have liked Velma. She had a perpetual smile on her face and a lilt in her voice that was not the least bit phony. It was just her. She wore a house dress that was pink floral print and had a matching belt. Her hair was cut short and was a beautiful salt and pepper color and permed into a little airy cap on her head. She had rosy cheeks and bright blue eyes and Darla could see Maggie's face in hers.

She asked some questions about Darla's parents and she caught the note of pride in Darla's voice when she spoke of them. Darla shared that her mother's sister lived nearby and that she had grown up with not only her two brothers, but the seven children from that family. She said her mother was known for her ability to use plants to help with healing and Velma was very interested in hearing about it. They had talked for an hour before Mrs. Wright's husband, Bill, stuck his head in the back door and said, "I cannot smell any sausage cooking!" He laughed and smiled at the women.

Velma said, "We are working for you Darla. Just tell Maggie and I how to do things."

Darla felt pride swell up in her. She had spent this first year in Washington feeling like she did not fit in and that she was probably very inadequate in comparison to all the other women in the Valley. But today, in Velma Wright's kitchen she felt very important.

She told Velma to start frying up two pounds of ground sausage. She said be sure you crumble it up good; too big of chunks and you got less grease for the gravy and less flavor. She asked Maggie to get her a good sized bowl so she could start mixing the biscuits. She had never really measured but she tried to be more precise as they watched her. Fat, flour, salt, baking powder and buttermilk was all it took. The amounts needed to add up to a good crumbly dough that could be manipulated into a smooth ball of dough once you added the buttermilk. She flattened it out on the floured countertop with her hands, making a big round circle. She had brought her own biscuit cutter, which her Ma had stuck in her bag when she left home. Once they were on the cookie sheets, she covered them with a tea towel while she started on the gravy.

First, she took out the cooked sausage crumbles and put them in a big serving bowl. She showed them how to add shortening (or lard) to get enough fat to make enough gravy to feed a table full of men. Then she took a fork and mixed in flour so that the fat became a nice paste and let it bubble and brown in the skillet. It was a nice big cast iron skillet and she had made sure that Velma had one before she came over. Then once it was browned and bubbly she slowly poured in milk and stirred and stirred, not letting a single lump form. Velma stood close to her as she did this and said, "Maggie, get over here and watch this. You know you have to be able to make this for Arlan."

When it was just the right thickness and the flour was cooked fully, Darla salted and peppered it to taste before she added the sausage back in. Velma commented that she used a lot of pepper and Darla said, "I guess Missourians like pepper. Youense will see, Arlan will add more when it comes to the table."

Velma fried eggs and Maggie set the table. Darla had brought a little bag of things and she pulled out a jar of black strap molasses that she had brought from home. She showed Velma how they liked to mix it with butter and then slather it on a biscuit without gravy. They put it all on the table and called the men in to eat.

Bill Wright sat at the head of the table in the Wright's dining room with Velma at one side of him, Maggie, then Arlan, Bryce at the other end, then Darla and Jake. Mr. Wright said a modified version of grace. It was "good food, good meat, good God, let's eat." Darla beamed as everyone complimented the breakfast. Velma said the biscuits were the lightest she had ever eaten and Bill said, "I was going to say that, but I just couldn't find time to stop shoving food in my mouth, it is so good."

It was a nice meal and there were many more like this in the years ahead. Darla always looked back on that meal as the first time she felt truly happy in the Yakima Valley. But there were going to be some changes in her life that would bring her back to this table many times.

Randall was having his dinner that day over at Carol's house with her folks. Carol's father was a doctor in Zillah and he only had the two children, Carol and her younger brother James. Randall was always surprised at how small some of the families were in the Valley. He was used to bigger families, at least four or five children at the minimum. But two were pretty common out here in the west. But of course, not if you were a catholic, as Carol's father had explained to him.

Carol's mother was a real socialite in the area. Her name was Coreen and she had many dinner parties and afternoon teas for the upper crust of her town. Although the town was small, there always are some people who feel superior to others, usually because they have a little more money or a bigger house or whatever. Doctor Gregory Simpson was a big deal in many ways. He was on the school board, President of the Eagles in Toppenish, Deacon at the Nazarene church and everybody in town's doctor. His wife Coreen was quite proud of all these facts. In fact she had a lot of ideas about her daughter Carol, including whom she should marry and when she should marry. On the top of her list was not a hillbilly from Missouri who had the unfortunate name of Podrick.

When Carol announced that she was dating him, she tried to soften the blow by calling him Randall and telling her parents he was very polite. Her brother James had already met him down at the garage one day when he was stopping in to talk to Jake. He introduced him as Pod and James laughed about it at the dinner table that night. "Can you imagine a name like Pod? What kind of hillbilly nonsense is that?"

Carol met Randall at a local dance that the

Lion's Club had put on for the harvest season. He was a good looking man and he watched her all evening before he stepped over and asked her to dance. She loved the way he said, "Miss, I was watchin' you dance and I was thinkin' I sure would like to try and keep up with ya."

Carol had flaming red hair and she always wore red lipstick and had on red fingernail polish. Even though her mother always told her to "tone it down dear", she liked red and that evening she had on a red blouse and a black skirt with red cherries around the hem. She really was a stunning girl.

There were many boys hovering around, but most of them had been scared off by her mother or their own mothers. Things were said about redheads being, "too flashy," "you will be marrying her mother," "she will expect you to be rich," etc. Carol was aware of these things and as much as she hated it, she could not seem to find a man to tough it out. She was nineteen and wanted to be married.

But when Randall stepped up, she thought he was just the right man to stand up to her parents and set her up with a house and children, because that is all she had ever wanted in her life. So she danced with him the rest of the night and shamelessly flirted with him the whole time.

He asked her to accompany him to a semiformal party that was happening out at the Grange Hall in a few weeks. She said yes. They walked into that dance arm in arm, with Randall wearing dress pants, a white shirt, and a bollo tie that had a silver long horned steer head on it. He had on shiny black cowboy boots and a nice plaid jacket. Carol was smashing in a black velvet, full skirted dress with a red sweater with sequins sewn on it. Her heels were red and everyone was staring at her. But she could not stop looking up at Randall.

Her mother fussed and said he was not good enough. Her brother made fun of everything he said, even the way he ate. "I have never seen someone pour coffee into a saucer to drink it. He is a real hillbilly. Does he do that in a restaurant too?"

Carol just glared at her brother and said, "He is the nicest person I have ever dated; I can tell you that and I don't care how he drinks coffee. You can just clam up James."

Coreen turned to her husband for support. "Gregory, can you please say something? Carol is going to throw herself away on a stupid hick from Missouri. He speaks oddly and for God's sakes, his real name is Podrick! I just don't think we want to send out wedding invitations with the name Podrick printed on them. What kind of name is that anyway?"

Doctor Gregory Simpson smoked a pipe and

he took a long draw off of it and said in his quiet way, "Carol, what is it that makes you think this Podrick fellow is the right person for you?"

This type of thing just irritated Coreen. The doctor was always so calm and collected. She wanted to throw something at him. But Carol smiled sweetly and said, "Daddy, he is so nice and polite. He treats me like a princess and he works hard at his job. He is getting a better job working for the Reclamation Bureau on the Roza Canal installing concrete pipelines and other things and he starts in a few weeks. I think he will take such good care of me and he wants little babies, just like I want! He said we can have as many as we want. I just love him Daddy."

Doctor Simpson looked at his wife and his son and said to Darla, "If this young man wants to ask me for your hand in marriage, I will say yes."

Coreen burst into tears and James said, "Great, now I have to watch him drink coffee in a saucer forever!"

Lucky for Randall, Doctor Simpson always had the last word in that family.

CHAPTER 23

Clear Out

The day that Muriel brought Darla home was a dark day for the Missourians. When Ralph came home, Muriel met him at the back door and said they needed to have a talk outside. She shut the door behind her and lead him back to the garden. She looked upset and Ralph was worried. She said, "Darla is in the house Ralph and she has been beaten, by Jake."

Ralph clinched his fists and said, "Goddamnit, goddamnit, I was so damn worried this would happen. Pod told me that he has a temper and he comes from bad men and goddamnnit, I just don't know, goddamnit."

Muriel was nodding her head and she said, "I know Ralph and I know that Pod and Arlan are not going to take this news well. I don't know what we can do, but I am not allowing her to go back there. She's got a little baby to take care of and I am telling you Ralph, she just isn't saying a word. Nothing. She's just staring straight ahead with big tears rolling down her beautiful little face."

Ralph stood still for a minute and then said, "I need to see her." He walked in the back door to find Darla sitting at the kitchen table, giving little Rosie her bottle and rocking back and forth. The swollen eye was purple and her lip was cut. He saw that Muriel had put a butterfly bandage on it, trying to keep it from needing to be stitched up. Her little arms were bruised too. But the worse thing was that faraway look in her eyes. It was like she had left and gone away. She was in total shock.

Ralph sat down across from her and said, "Hello there Darla. I am going to go and get your brother and your cousin and we are going to talk about what needs to be done. You stay right here with Muriel and she will help you. You can stay here just as long as you need to. And if Jake comes down that driveway, Muriel knows how to use the shot gun. Muriel, get some shells out of my drawer and if he comes, shoot right over the top of his head. If he keeps coming, shoot his knee."

That was the first time Darla looked up and

she said, "I dunno ifen youense has to shoot him. He probably won't come anyways."

Ralph shook his head and looked at Muriel and she nodded and he was out the door. In about an hour he was back with Randall and Arlan. He had only told them a little, just that Jake had hit Darla and she was at his house safe. Randall grabbed his head in his hands and burst right into tears. That was Randall, he could cry and he did when he felt like it. Arlan was silent but his fists were balled up tight and he found himself holding his breath.

It was much worse when they saw Darla. Randall fell to his knees in front of her and said, "Oh my baby girl, oh my baby girl. I is supposed to be takin' care of you. I jest cain't stand it." He was wracked with sobs and put his arms around her and baby Rose. Arlan stood stock still and could not speak. He had only seen a woman beaten one time and that was when he had seen Jake's Ma sitting at his Mama's kitchen table while she and Aunt Lutie were doctoring her face. He remembered how scared and sad she looked and how carefully Aunt Lutie was wiping away the blood.

He knew Aunt Lutie feared that same thing would happen to Darla and now it had. He felt like he had let his Aunt Lutie down too. He was madder than hell. Madder than he had been at Abel when he took his horse, madder than when the Caster boys chased him and beat him. He was red faced and hard bodied and he wanted to kill Jake Wright.

Muriel thought it would be good if Darla took a rest and the baby was asleep so it was a good time to put her down on the spare bed. She tucked a quilt around her and kissed her on her forehead. Darla smiled at her and said, "Thank ya."

Muriel walked back into the kitchen to hear what was being said by the men. Randall had composed himself and he was talking about driving over to talk to Jake and let him know he was a dead man walking. Arlan wanted to call him over to Randall's place and when he got out of the car, jump him and drag him into the chicken pen and tie him up and just let the chickens shit all over him and peck him while they decided what to do with him. Ralph said they could call the sheriff, but he did not think they would do anything. He said he had seen it before. They always tell the woman to go home and stop making her old man so mad. He was leaning toward the chicken pen idea. Muriel said she thought they should make him wonder where she was and not talk to him until tomorrow. Then she thought they should go down to the garage where he worked and tell his boss that he was going to be off work for a while because he beat the hell out of his wife and now, they needed to beat him.

Muriel pulled out cold roast beef and made sandwiches and set a lemon cake on the table so they could eat while they planned. She brought out a jug of cold milk and poured each of them a big glass. This kind of talk was making them hungry.

After about an hour they heard a car pull in and it was Jake. All three of the men jumped up and were about to run out the door, but Muriel said, "Stop. Sit down. Let's make him come in and face all of us."

They sat down, but it was hard. He knocked on the back door before he came in and when he saw Randall, Arlan and Ralph seated at the table with Muriel standing beside them he hesitated to come in. He said, "Howdy. Ah, I was a lookin' for Darla. I reckoned she was over here with Muriel. Youense seen her?"

Randall stood up then and said in that calm and strong voice he used when he was good and mad. "Well, we has seen her Jake. We seen her black eye and her split lip and we saw that she has been pushed around and bruised up. Yes, we seen her. But you (and he poked Jake in the chest as hard as his finger could) ain't seein' her again."

Jake stepped back and said, "Well, I is her man and she is comin' home with me. You ain't got no right keepin' me from her. That ain't the way things is done and you knowed it."

Randall laughed in his face and said, "You ain't seen anythin' like we plan to do to you."

Jake turned and ran out to the car and was gone in a quick second. Ralph said, "That was great Randall. You scared the shit out of him. He is going to be running for a long time!"

Arlan sat down hard and said, "We gotta get 'im now. How we gonna do it?"

Just then Darla walked back into the kitchen. She was holding Rose and she had obviously heard it all. She said, "I knowed how to get him home. Tell him I will be there."

The plan was hatched at Muriel and Ralph's kitchen table. The next morning Ralph would call Jake and tell him that he was going to bring Darla and the baby home. He said they would get there about 7:00 a.m. When they got there, Randall and Arlan would be in the back seat. Darla would walk into the house and tell Jake he needed to go and get her suitcase. When he came out, Randall and Arlan would be waiting by the back door. They would drag him to the car and stuff him in the back seat between them. Then they would drive him out to Randall's place and put him in the chicken pen, tied up, and tell him what their plans were for him.

The plans were for him to get in his car and drive back to Missouri. He could take some clothes and his last paycheck, but he could not take Darla and Rose. They would be staying right where they were and Arlan would move in with them and take care of them as long as they needed it.

They told him he could not come back to Washington to see Darla and Rose. They told him he could not go and see any of their family in Missouri. They told him they would kill him if he did not do what they told him, period.

Darla would be packing his bag while they kept him out at the coop and Ralph would drive in and pick it up. Muriel would come over in her car and drive Jake's car out to him. She would first stop and fill up the gas tank at the garage and let them know Jake was returning to Missouri. She would even pick up his last paycheck.

It was a plan and it satisfied all of them. They would let Jake know that a shot gun was going to be loaded at every back door he might try to go to. That included Missouri, where they would make a phone call to Lulu at the store and let her in on what was going to happen. Now to carry it out.

That was not hard. It went so smooth that Arlan said that maybe they should go into robbing banks or some other criminal activity. When Ralph brought Muriel back to spend the night with Darla, she was sitting at the table crocheting a little hat for Rose and she said to Muriel, "I been scared since I married him. I ain't gonna be scared no more."

But that was not the last of Jake Wright. He made it to the Oregon border and his pride and his bravado got the best of him. He made a fateful decision to return to get his wife and baby.

CHAPTER 24

Dark Times

It had been about a month since they had run him out of town. Jake pulled into town in the dead of the night. He had traded his car in a place called Kennewick and picked up a truck that was older and not much like what you would expect Jake to be driving.

He parked down at the river and slept in his truck until the first rays of sunshine hit the Yakima River and bounced off the round rocks lining the shore. He drove into town and parked about a block from his house and scrunched down in the seat until he saw Arlan pull away, headed to work. Arlan was working for the highway department now, so he had normal hours and good pay and could sleep at home every night; the home that was Jake's.

When he saw Arlan drive away, he rolled the truck to a spot across the street from his house and made his way to the back door. He looked in to see Darla washing up breakfast at the sink. She was singing under her breath and swaying in a way that made Jake hungry for her. He slipped open the door and snuck up behind her. He put his hand over her mouth and he could feel the scream coming. He leaned over and said into her ear, "You jest settle down Darla. I ain't gonna hurt ya none." He spun her around and saw the terror in her eyes.

For a moment he regretted that look in her eyes. He missed the one that was full of love and caring, but he knew they had gone beyond that and if all he could get was terror, then he would be fine. He whispered, "Youense pack yer bag and Rosie's too. We are headin' outta here now. Don't even try to scream darlin' or it will be yer last."

Darla shook all over and he shoved her toward the bedroom and stood as she packed a suitcase hurriedly, throwing in whatever she could, not even thinking. He followed her to the baby's room and watched her throwing diapers and little sleepers into another suitcase. She was crying the whole time, no sound, and little Rose did not wake up.

He followed her into the kitchen where she

put bottles and nipples in a bag and grabbed a bib. She turned in circles trying to think what she should bring and she started to bend at the knees to collapse on the floor. Jake jerked her up and said, "Get yerself together here Darla." He pushed her and the baby out of the back door and walked them to his truck. He threw the bags in the back and hopped in and drove them out of town.

Thank God for caring neighbors, because the neighbors across the street, the Hazelton's, were a retired couple. They were always watching out for the comings and goings at the Wright's. In fact they had watched her leaving with Muriel that day with her black eye and bloody lip and they were glad to see Arlan move in. Mr. Hazelton saw Jake enter the back door and he told his wife he was going to call Ralph and Muriel's house to tell them that "that sneaky no-good son of a bitch" is back.

Muriel answered the phone and Ralph had just left to go out to the orchard. He had 50 acres of apples and 50 acres of pears going now with his father and he was always busy doing something. Today he was mowing, so he would be on the tractor all day. Muriel jumped in the car and sped out to the orchard to catch Ralph at the end of a row of trees. He could tell something was wrong and he shut off the tractor as she came running toward him.

Ralph told her to go over to the Reclamation Bureau office and ask them to get in touch with Randall Taylor, working on the Roza Division. Randall had been working for them for a while now and was working on laying the underground pipelines made of concrete that took the canal water underground instead of depending on open ditches. They laid the pipe 18" down and it was hard work, but Randall felt rewarded, knowing that farmers could get their water in a more efficient way.

Meanwhile, Ralph drove over to talk to Mr. Hazelton to get the facts about the truck and when they pulled out. He was standing in the yard at Darla's when Randall pulled up, followed shortly by Arlan. Both men had never taken a day off work in their lives, but when they said to their bosses their sister was in trouble and might get killed, they told them to get going.

The three men decided to split up. Ralph was sure that Jake was going to try and take her to another state and hide her, so he said he would drive straight toward the Oregon border. Randall thought Arlan should stay put to handle anything that might come up locally and he said he would drive east. They did not have much of a plan, but they knew they had to try to find her fast or they might lose her for good. Everybody had a shotgun on the front seat and for Arlan, at the backdoor. They agreed to check in at 5:00 by calling Ralph's house and telling Muriel where they were.

It was a long day for everyone. Maggie came to Darla's when she got off work to wait with Arlan. Muriel sat by the phone and Carol came over to keep her company. She and Randall were getting married in August and she had been so busy planning the wedding, she really had not realized how horrible the situation with Darla and Jake had become.

Maggie called her father and he said he would be glad to go mow the orchard for Ralph. Her brother Bryce said he would go feed the chickens at Randall's place and make sure the garden was watered. Doctor Simpson said if anyone needed a doctor, it would be free of charge. Coreen Simpson turned to her son James and said, "See, these hillbillies cause all kinds of problems."

No one saw them that day or for the next few. Ralph and Randall came home and everyone was frantically trying to figure out what to do. Mrs. Hazelton had written down the license plate and Ralph had gone over to the police chief's house to see what they could do to help them.

The police chief was known as Big Burt Brown or Big Burt or BB by his wife. He was as round as a barrel but was fast on his feet and known to be a great mediator. He scolded

Ralph for not telling him sooner, but he made some calls and got the State Troopers looking for them. They found them.

Jake had rented a little motel room for them in a town called Chewelah over in eastern Washington, up north of Spokane. He had decided to take his family north to Canada. He had underestimated the will of Randall and Arlan to get Darla back and the motel was right on the main road and his truck was parked with his license plate facing the road. It was about 6 a.m. when a State Trooper knocked at the door and said, "I am here to check on the welfare of Darla and Rose Wright." Jake started to say they were not with him when Darla slipped under his arm and threw herself at the State Trooper.

Her hair was matted from the broken window on the truck and the wind whipping it for two days. Her dress was ripped and she had a swollen jaw and her arm was hanging funny, like it was broken. She held a baby girl with her good arm. Her eyes were wild with fear and the State Trooper pushed her behind him and told Jake to put his hands up.

Jake went to jail for assault and battery in the jail down in Spokane because he had committed the crime, according to Darla, alongside a road in what they thought must have been Spokane County. Ralph and Randall drove to

Spokane to a motel that the State Trooper's had put Darla and Rose in and picked them up. Randall held her in his arms and said, "This here ain't never gonna happen again, never, ever, never."

When they got back to Zillah, everyone was waiting at Ralph and Muriel's for them to return. Muriel, Carol, and Maggie fussed over Darla and the baby. They got Darla to take a nice bath and called Doctor Simpson to come out and look her over to see if she needed attention. She did and he set her arm sitting at Muriel's kitchen table in one of Muriel's dresses, which was too big and her hair was in a towel. She did not scream or cry even though it had to hurt as it had been broken a few days. He made a cast right there and then and put it in a sling. Her other injuries were going to heal, but he gave her some pain pills to help with the pain of the swollen jaw. He looked baby Rose over and thank God she was fine except for a slight rash as Darla had run out of clean diapers before they got far.

Muriel and Ralph insisted that everyone stay and have dinner and she made a big ham dinner, while Carol and Maggie helped her in the kitchen. Maggie was crying quietly and each time she looked at Darla, she cried harder. Carol was very calm, like her father, and she made sure that the baby's diaper rash was attended to. She took over the care of Rose for a few days as Darla was having a hard time doing everything with one arm.

The safety and the love that was there in Ralph's house was something that Darla would never forget. She had loved Muriel from the start, but now she thought she was the best woman, next to her Mama, that she had ever known. Muriel was different than Mama in that she was a hugger and a kisser, just like Ralph. She wrapped her arms around Darla often and told her she loved her and told her she could live with them if she wanted. They would make room for her and Rose.

No one thought she should go back to the house in town. It just had too many bad memories and it was where Jake would always come to find her. So things moved a long very quickly as everyone planned for the future.

Jake never turned up in Washington again. Once he got out of jail, he hitch hiked back to Missouri to see what he could find there at home. It was Lulu, Rayleen, and Ticky who ended up dealing with him. It was September when he showed up and it was a weekday, so Lulu was at work. Uncle Orvil was gone to Springfield with a neighbor to look at yet another horse and Rayleen and Ticky were busy canning apple butter.

It was still hot out and the yard had dried up

except for where Rayleen threw the dish water on the front flower beds. There was no breeze to speak of and Rayleen had her hair pulled up on top of her head and was wearing a sleeveless dress. Ticky had started wearing pants a few years ago and she had cut off the legs of an old pair of Pod's she found in the attic. In fact, most of her clothes were Pod and Basil's old clothes that Aunt Lutie had saved to make quilts and blankets. Ticky had on a work shirt with the sleeves cut out and her hair was in braids pinned to the top of her head. She was barefoot and so was Rayleen.

They heard someone walking on the dry grass out front and Rayleen hollered, "Howdy. Whose that?" She caught her breath when Jake stuck his head in the door. Ticky went out the back door before he could see her and got one of the horses out of the barn and took off for Noble to get Lulu.

Jake said, "Well, howdy Ms. Rayleen. Youense are lookin' mighty fine these days. You got a glass of cold water fer a traveler?"

Rayleen looked him up and down and said calmly, "Ifen you aim to hit me, Jake Wright, ya gotta 'nother think comin'. I ain't no punchin' bag for a no good man like you."

Jake chuckled and said, "Now Rayleen honey, I ain't gonna hit ya! But, ifen I was, ya would be long dead afore anyone got here to save ya."

Rayleen reached for the shotgun by the back door. She took bullets out of her apron pocket because they had all been ready since they heard he got cut loose from jail. She put the shells in and snapped the shotgun shut and turned and pointed it at Jake. "Now, now, there ain't no reason fer that! I ain't fixin' to hurt ya. I jest got some questions to ask ya, that's all."

Rayleen kept the gun pointed at him and said, "You got five minutes to ask."

Jake stretched his long legs under the kitchen table and looked around the room, like he was trying to decide where to begin. Then he said in the meanest, vilest voice he could speak in, "You know, youense might be here livin' off old' Orvil now, but when that ol' man kicks the bucket, this place is goin' to my Darla and Pod. Youense will jest be kicked out then and we will see who is so high and mighty then."

Rayleen did not react. She jest kept the gun steady and in a few minutes a car came tearing into the driveway. Lulu was standing in the kitchen with Mr. Burns right beside her in seconds. She nodded approval at Rayleen and she said, "Jake Wright, git yer ass down the road and don't youense ever come back here. If Orvil sees ya, yer a dead man and no one can help ya."

Mr. Burns stepped farther into the room and said, "Youense might as well git the hell out of this whole area. No one wants youense here, not even yer family. We all knowed what you did and we want youense outta Ozark County and Douglas County and all of Missouri. Ifen ya don't go, someone is gonna kill ya. Ya hear me?"

Jake stood up and tried to laugh, but Lulu could see he was actually scared now. So she went on, "Jake, youense better go far away, like St. Louis or Chicago or somewheres where no one knowed ya. You is gonna git killed here and that ain't no joke."

Jake walked out like he was not scared, but they all saw that his hands were shaking. Rayleen followed him out, never putting the shot gun down. When Jake pulled out of their driveway Ticky came flying down the road on her horse, Mission. Her braids were flying behind her and she jumped off mid–trot. "He gone?"

"Yes, he's gone." Lulu smiled at Rayleen, Mr. Burns and Ticky and said, "I am perty sure that we ain't gonna see ol' Jake no more."

They decided not to tell Uncle Orvil. He had been ready to drive to Washington and find Jake and kill him since they had received news of his treatment of Darla. They had kept him under control, or so they thought. What they did not know is that he had taken a little trip over to see Jake's Pa. They did not know that he had brought Uncle Elmer a long too and the three old men had a real heart to heart on

Jake's old man's front lawn. It seems that Jake's Pa had lost an ear somehow that day and Doc Frederick's could not get him to say how it happened, but if he would have looked hard, he would have found it in the driveway where Orvil had chucked it.

Big Families

As things moved a long in the Yakima Valley the Zillah/Missouri family grew. Randall and Carol had five boys in about ten years. They were happy as could be, living on a nice place just outside of town with a big two story farmhouse surrounded by gardens and pig pens, big shady trees. Much to Carol's mother's dismay, she enjoyed being pregnant and she was so proud of her brood of boys. When she brought them over to Doctor Simpson and Coreen's house, they ran amuck, opening cupboards, putting on their Grandpa's stethoscope, eating them out of house and home. Coreen acted like she just dreaded their visits, but deep down she admired Carol for her calm collected way of raising a herd of boys. Carol never shouted, but the boys knew her word was final. She stood there with her flaming red hair and managed them with authority. It reminded Coreen of how much Carol was like her father.

The boys were all big guys, except for the middle one, Joey. Somehow, he had inherited what Randall called "my Aunt Letty Anne's tiny little frame" and he got teased some. But having two older brothers and two younger brothers that could whip anyone was to his advantage.

Randall beamed when he saw the boys pouring out of the house when he came home from work. He beamed when Carol's belly stuck straight out under her smocks and he loved to watch her maneuver around the kitchen like it was not a problem. But it was not all paradise at their house. Things got messy when Arlan and Randall decided to go in on some farmland together.

Arlan and Maggie were married by then and they had three little boys and one little girl. They had been living in a small house in town and it just was not what Arlan had dreamed of when he came to the Valley. He saw a place for sale in the country that was a nice rambler sitting in the middle of an apple orchard and it had a view of Mt. Adams through the big picture window in the front. He came home and told Maggie all about it and they sat down to do the math and it just did not look good. Maggie no longer worked as she had her hands full with a house full of children. The house was too small to hold all of them and they were stacked up in the second bedroom, with her oldest two sleeping on the sofa bed in the living room. She said she could ask her father for help, but he had already helped Darla and Bryce get a place and her mother had told her they really did not have the money, but they felt so strongly about all that Darla had been through, they did it anyway.

Yes, Darla and Bryce became an item. He was three years younger than her and when he was about seventeen, he found himself stopping by to see her and Rose in the little house they had in town. Darla had a job at Stadelman's Fruit warehouse during cherry, prune, and apple harvest. Rose stayed with Muriel while she worked. She could afford the rent on the little house, but not much more.

Bryce made excuses to go there all the time. He picked up a load of cantaloupe from a farmer or a box of tomatoes or he bought a nice ham to take over. Darla thought he was so cute, but she never imagined that she would date him, as she was once divorced (sort of) and was twenty years old. But slowly things changed and Bryce became a permanent fixture there. He stayed until late at night and when he graduated high school and went to work at the Toppenish Sale Yard, he asked her to marry him.

Darla said she could not. "Bryce, I have never been divorced from Jake. I am not sure where he is and I don't want to know. I cannot marry you." Darla's accent was still there but she had mimicked the way Carol and Maggie and Muriel spoke to tone down her colloquial speech.

Bryce smiled his big smile, which always made him look like he was twelve years old and said, "Nobody knows that, Darla. We can just say we went up to Yakima and got a license and had a judge marry us. We can take Arlan and Maggie with us and they will not tell a soul. I want to be your husband and that is all there is to it. I do not care if it is legal or not. It will be real to us." And so, that was how they became Mr. and Mrs. Bryce Jones.

Back to Arlan and Maggie's dilemma. Arlan thought about it and decided he would speak with Randall. They had always kept an eye out for each other since they had moved to Washington. Arlan had helped pay for Randall's tractor so he could help him with plowing up the field he had purchased next to his place. He had helped rebuild the barn and paid for some of the lumber, just because he had the money at the time.

They had both helped Darla when Jake first left and paid her rent until she could get some work. It was just what they did, sharing everything and borrowing whatever they needed.

So, Arlan asked Randall if he would go out and look at the place with him one evening. They drove out of town and up on the plateau that had a nice view of Mt. Adams and Mt. Rainier. He pulled into the yard of the house, which was currently empty and the two of them got out and looked around. It was a nice house for sure; brick with big windows facing the mountains. It had a garage and a shop out back and there was a small apple orchard surrounding it. The owners had been moved out due to old age and their children lived in Seattle, so they wanted to sell it all; ladders, tractor, picking buckets, tools, furniture, everything. The price was good, but the down payment was where Arlan was going to need some help. He told Randall that this would be a good chance for him to get some farming done and still keep his job. He offered Randall half the profits for five years if he could muster up some money to help him put a good down payment on it.

It did not take any convincing. Randall said, "I been hopin' youenses would get a place like this. Be perfect for them boys to run wild and you need to do some farmin', I agree. I can help ya with the money. I got enough saved to give you more than half, I would say."

Arlan smiled big and said, "We can split profits and share equipment and once you plant your ground in alfalfa, I can help you get the hay mower and bailer. I jest cain't tell you how much this will help us. I jest cain't thank ya enough."

Randall put his arm on Arlan's shoulder and said, "Youense is a brother to me Arlan. Ya always have been and ya always will be."

These agreements between the cousins never did get passed by the women. It was not something that they felt obligated to share. They were used to being in charge of the big decisions and asking their wives if they were willing to go along with it just was not something they would ever think to do.

Carol found out that Randall was helping when she saw him writing a check at the kitchen table one night. The boys were bathed and in bed and she was just sitting down to rest when she spotted him hunched over at the table. "What are you doing Randall?"

He did not answer for a minute as he was checking his spelling and if he had written the numbers out correctly. Then he looked up and said, "Oh, I am writin' a check for Arlan. He's gettin' a new place up on the Roza and I am helpin' with the down payment."

Carol leaned over his shoulder to see the

amount and she gasped. "That is a lot of money Randall. That is more than we paid down for this place!"

Randall looked at her and frowned and said, "Well, prices go up and besides, Arlan is like my brother. We been helpin' each other ever since we came to Washington."

Carol sat down and stared at Randall and said, "This is not Missouri Randall. People need to make their own way. We cannot keep helping Arlan and Darla and keep up with what our boys need. You are so used to living like a clan of hillbillies, honey. There really is no need to do that anymore."

Randall had never said a cross word to Carol since he married her 12 years before. In fact, he was sensitive to her mother and brother's dislike of him and he tried hard to "fit in", but this comment about a clan of hillbillies was hurtful.

He stood up and pushed his chair out and put the check in his pocket and walked to the door to leave. He turned around and said, "Carol, I might come from a clan of hillbillies, but I ain't never said anything hurtful to youense or yer kin. I have put up with your brother's smart mouth and your mother rollin' her eyes and I jest keep turnin' the other cheek. But by God, I am helpin' Arlan and Maggie and that is final."

He left the house and he did not come back when it was time for bed. He did not come back when it was midnight. In fact, Carol did not see him until the next day after he got home from work. He came in the house and acted like nothing had happened. Carol was ready to fight with him, but he simply said, "Did the boys feed the hogs this mornin'?"

Carol nodded yes and he stepped into the bathroom and washed up for supper. Carol watched him from the kitchen. She was always fascinated by his routine. He scrubbed himself up like she had never seen any other man do. He got the soap into a big lather and rubbed it all over his face, his neck, in his ears, up his arms and through his fingers. Then he splashed hot water all over his face and hands and rinsed it all off. Next, he took a big towel, not a hand towel, and rubbed himself shiny clean. Then he combed his hair to the side with a neat part. This was his nightly routine. He taught this to the boys as they each got old enough and they had to pass inspection before they could sit down at their mother's table.

That was the end of Carol commenting on the farming practices of her husband and Arlan. It was not that she did not resent it and she made it known in many small ways, especially to Maggie, but it did not change a thing.

Maggie understood Arlan and Randall a little better, but she too was always amazed when Randall pulled in and loaded up some tools or she saw her wheelbarrow leave in his truck. She once told her father, "Daddy, they just borrow everything and they never even ask. It seems like they all feel like "what's yours is mine".

Bill Jones chuckled and said, "I think it is just the way of the Missourians. My friend over in Toppenish is from Missouri and he and his brother do that same thing. Maybe where they came from they did not have much, so you shared whatever you did have... I don't know honey."

Maggie was standing there with her little baby girl, Patsy Anne, on her hip. She had birthed three boys and although she loved them dearly, she was thrilled when she got a little girl. Patsy Anne wore dresses and bonnets every day. She was such a cute little girl and Arlan said she looked just like his sister Toady. Her hair was auburn red and curled around her beautiful little face. She was tiny like Letty Anne had been and her eyes were blue and bright. Arlan was crazy about her and packed her around all the time. Maggie knew it made him think about his sisters at home. Being the only boy in a houseful of girls made him a good father to a daughter.

The three boys were stair steps at ages eight, seven, and six. They were rough and tumble farm boys and they loved to play with Uncle Randall's boys whenever they could. When those boys were all together, it was a baseball team, a basketball team, a football team, or whatever else they could get themselves into.

Arlan's oldest boy, Wally, was crazy about horses, just like Uncle Orvil, and Arlan taught him everything he knew. Wally was breaking horses by the time he was twelve and riding from farm to farm with one or two little brothers hanging on behind him. The other two boys were Jess and Aaron and they were hunters. They both got BB guns for Christmas on the same year and they shot everything that moved, including each other, until Arlan had to whip them both.

Randall's five boys were Jim, John, Joe, Jack, and Jerry. Carol thought that would be so cute, but half the time Randall got their names mixed up and ended up just yelling, "You over there, come here and help out!" Her mother was forever complaining and said she should have at least named them James, Johnathan, Joseph, and Jerome. Jack was a horses name she said and it should have been eliminated altogether. Carol ignored her mother, as always, and she smiled and said things to her mother like, "I am so proud of my five Taylor boys."

Then there was Ralph and Muriel. They never were blessed with children. They tried always, but something was not quite right. In those days you just accepted the situation and no one went to the doctor for assistance. Muriel cried quietly each month that she was not pregnant and she embraced her friends and their little ones, but she never had the pleasure of being a mom.

Muriel did develop a special closeness to little Rose. She took care of her whenever she could and she even set up a little bedroom space for her with a pink canopy bed and toys on a shelf. Rose called her Gramma Muriel and Ralph was Papa Ralph. They doted over her and enjoyed having her live with them while she and Darla were recovering from the trauma of Jake.

When Darla and Bryce had a baby boy, Muriel took care of him too whenever Darla was working. His name was William, after Bryce's father, and he was a clone of Bryce, right down to the big cheesy grin on his face.

The Yakima/Missouri clan grew and they met other Missouri transplants in the Valley. They found a church where most of them would attend (except Randall and Arlan, who said farming was more important) and of course it was Baptist like back home. They had a picnic each summer and called it the Missouri Picnic and the amount of food was mouthwatering. People showed up from all over the Valley and some came as from as far as Oregon to meet up and talk about home and laugh and eat food that they all grew up enjoying.

Carol and Muriel and Maggie always attended and they became friends with some of the women, but there was always just a little difference between them and the Missouri girls. It was not easy to pin down. Maybe there was a lot of laughing when the Missouri women got together and lots of recollections about home. The Washington women did not have those memories, but they had been raised to be polite and they nodded and smiled as the Missouri women bent over at the waist laughing so hard.

One time Darla said to Maggie, "I knowed you don't think you is better than me, but I think some of the other gals from home might think you do."

Maggie spun around and looked at Darla and said, "Are you kidding me? What makes them think that?"

Darla smiled and said, "You speak so nicely and you always look so put together. You can't help it Maggie, you are just so pretty and so smart."

Maggie laughed out loud and said, "Well, I would never have guessed that Darla! I better start acting snooty since I am so smart and pretty!"

The two girls giggled. They were close. When Maggie's little brother Bryce said he wanted to marry Darla, Maggie burst into tears and told him, "She is such a wonderful person. I am just so happy if she is going to be my sister-in-law. She will be the sister I didn't have!"

As the children of Randall and Carol, Arlan and Maggie, and Bryce and Darla moved through the Zillah school system, they were their own force to be reckoned with. There were nine boys and two girls and they were on every sporting team or cheerleading squad or homecoming court for quite a few years. The boys were mostly athletic, the girls were beauties and the parents cheered them on.

There were times that there was not harmony. Sometimes the boys got into some fights with each other that ended with bloody noses or black eyes. Sometimes one of them would try to date the other cousin's girlfriend. Sometimes the women would get mad at each other over who was lazy and did not bring enough food to the gatherings or who cut her hair in the same hairdo as hers. Once Arlan brought Randall's oldest boy a dog that bit him and Carol had a meltdown that included her mother getting involved and Maggie calling her father and it was a mess.

Then there was a crop dispute. Randall had planted his additional thirty acres in alfalfa for several years, but he had decided to grow a crop of mint. It was a fairly new crop in the Valley and people were seeing some good profits. His field got a good shade in the afternoon and it had not helped his alfalfa crop much, but he talked with one of the Washington State Extension agents and he suggested mint.

The alfalfa crop had enriched the soil somewhat. The mint needed moisture with good drainage and his field had that. He also needed to purchase some geese for weeding the mint. This is where the trouble started.

Bryce worked at the Toppenish Sale Yard and although their primary market was cattle, horses, hogs and some sheep, occasionally flocks of geese or chickens came up for sale along with an occasional goat. He was put in charge of securing the geese.

Arlan would do the planting as he had a nicer tractor than Randall and he had time on a Saturday to plant the field. Randall and Bryce were there too, just because this was a new crop and it required lots of conversations and speculation with the men. Carol was called on to make a nice big lunch, which she did not really want to do. She was not feeling so well that spring and had a case of bunions on her feet that was quite painful. She was wearing slippers most of the time and her feet ached when she stood too long. But Randall was really not so sympathetic about it. He had been raised with Lutie and Letty Anne as role models and he could not remember them complaining or sitting down any given day of their lives, except when they were dying. So, he just hollered into the kitchen after breakfast when he was pulling on his boots, "Carol, hon, we are gonna need a nice big lunch today. Arlan and Bryce will be here. Maybe the Puckett boys too."

Carol sat down at the table and put her head in her hands. Randall did not see it because he was long gone at that point, but she was not crying. She was clenching her jaw and rubbing her temples. Her thoughts were jumbled and she did not know who she could turn to. She knew she could call Maggie and ask her to come and help prepare lunch. Maggie would come in a second. She knew she could call Darla too, but she was working a shift at Del Monte in the asparagus and she did not want to ask her as she knew she was tired. She just did not want to cook a giant lunch today. She was tired. Tired of cooking, washing, keeping five boys in line, raising a garden, paying the bills and worrying about all of it.

Randall made good money, but he spent it too. He liked to purchase things for the farm and more horses and another sow and a milk cow and whatever else took his fancy. He also loved to feed the family and he would invite everyone to their house on Sundays for big dinners. Carol liked to go to church and if she went, she was scrambling all afternoon to fix enough to feed her boys, Arlan's brood, and six or seven adults.

She could not talk to her Mother who was fond of saying things sarcastically, still. She would roll her eyes when she saw Carol's broken fingernails and wrinkled hands. "Wear rubber gloves for goodness sakes Carol." She would inspect the house every time she came and find dust bunnies and dirt in every corner. She said things like, "You should have listened to me Carol. You are now a full time laborer for a half ass Missouri farmer."

Carol's Father was better and he would come by and get the younger boys and take them fishing or hiking in the mountains. He praised Carol's hard work and told her to remember, this had been her dream. She leaned on his shoulder and tried not to cry. He took a close look at her feet and he let her know that surgery was an option, although it was painful and recovery meant staying off her feet. She just shook her head because she was unsure when staying off her feet would be an option.

On this Saturday when they were planting the peppermint, Bryce brought the geese out. It took 3 geese approximately per acre to keep the weeds down in the first month or two of new growth, but Randall thought ninety geese was too many so they settled on thirty five. The geese would eat any alfalfa that came up and all other grasses and weeds, but they did not like mint. You could keep them in the field for a few months and then they might start getting a taste for mint and you had to move them out.

They were not a wandering type of animal and liked to stay close together and would walk back to their pen in the evening to eat some corn and drink water. The pen had been built by Jim and John, their oldest two and it was situated behind the current barn and facing the field. It looked sturdy and the boys were excited and proud to put the geese in. They were in charge of feeding and caring for the geese.

So the geese were delivered and Carol made a huge lunch. She felt angry this day and so she decided she would not call Maggie and that she would be a martyr (though she would not see it this way) and make it all herself. After all, she did not have a daughter or anyone to help her. So she made a big pork roast that she had thawed out the day before. She made mashed potatoes and gravy and cooked corn she had frozen the summer before. She made a big batch of biscuits the way Darla had taught her too and she even whipped up a cherry pie using canned cherries from the year before. She cooked slices of ham and fried bacon, because she knew the Missouri men would go for the meat. She boiled up some eggs too and made some deviled eggs like her mother did for her luncheons. She did all this with aching feet and an anger that could have set off a bomb if someone lit a match to it.

That someone happened to be Randall. At noon he brought the crew in and it was a full house for sure. Arlan and his three boys, Randall, Bryce, Ralph, and their own five boys lined up to wash and took seats around the table. It held twelve, so there was a spot for everyone but Carol.

The table was laden with all of her cooking and she stood at the kitchen sink sipping a cup of coffee when she heard Randall say, "Hon, can you whip up some more gravy? We have jest about cleaned this here bowl."

Carol stood stock still and she started to boil like a kettle that had been sitting on the stove too long and starts to spill over. She slammed her coffee cup on the counter and she stepped into the dining room, holding onto a big spoon she used to dish up the mashed potatoes. She pointed the spoon at Randall and she spoke in a vicious tone, "No, hon, I will not make more gravy. I made plenty of damn gravy. I made plenty of damn food. I am not making any more food and furthermore, I am not cleaning up the mess you have made, so you can just shove it, all of you."

She stormed out the back door, grabbing her purse off the hook as she passed by it and drove away in her long blue Buick and headed for somewhere, anywhere but here on the farm with that ravenous group of men around the table.

Randall tried to make light of the situation and so did the older boys. They had seen their mother mad, but she usually did not act like that in front of people. The youngest boy Jerry started to cry and said, "Daddy, is she gonna come back?"

Randall chuckled and said, "Of course she is Jerry. She's just got hurtin' feet and it has made her cranky."

Bryce said, "I could clean up these dishes. My mother always made me do things like that. Jack and Jerry, you two can help me."

Randall started to protest but Arlan wisely said, "I think that is a good idea." He turned to his three and said, "Wally, Jess, Aaron, you pitch in too and it won't take so long."

Randall was embarrassed and quite upset. He did not think that Carol had any right to treat his family and friends that way. He was not happy seeing Bryce leading a crew in the kitchen. He looked at Ralph and said, "I jest ain't got any idea what I am s'pposed to do with that woman."

Ralph nodded and said, "Well, she is probably going into the change. Muriel is and it is a rocky road, let me tell you. With women they are either getting their monthly cycle, having morning sickness, or going into the change. It's a helluva a business trying to understand them."

Randall nodded and said, "I jest hope she comes back."

They went outside to resume the planting and talking when they noticed that the gate to the geese pen was wide open. Randall hollered, "Jim, John, git out here now! Them geese is loose."

The geese were over in the adjoining field helping themselves to a new crop of potatoes that had just been planted. They were hungry as they had not been fed for a day or two and they were destroying the rows as fast as they could go. The eight boys that were there ran through the potato field, smashing new growth and trying to get the geese back to their pen. Thirty five geese is a lot and they are not friendly. They hiss and lunge and they will bite you. Little Joe got bit on his legs and Jess was sure one bit his finger off. It was chaos.

Once they got them back in the pen, except for one lone goose who flopped over dead at the edge of the yard, a lot of yelling took place.

It had been a bad day for Randall already and he started screaming at his boys that they were useless as "geese farmers" and he got so angry that Ralph had to step in and say, "Randall, buddy, it was an accident. The boys did not mean it."

Randall was still ranting and raving when Little Joe said, "What's wrong with that goose John?"

The geese were dropping to the ground at an alarming rate. It seems that young white potato shoots are poison to geese and because they were so hungry, they just gorged on them. Geese were dropping until the entire flock was down and dead. The men and boys stood and stared at the pen full of dead birds. They were scratching their heads over that fiasco, when here came the neighbor whose potatoes had been ravaged. He was not a happy man.

His name was Earl Beam and he had been living on his place for forty five years, which is what he always said whenever someone talked to him. He started in right away, "In forty five years I have never had any trouble with neighbors until you, Randall Taylor from Missouri. I have had some idiots live by me but you take the cake. Those damn geese have ruined my potato crop and your pack of boys finished off anything the geese didn't get after."

Randall, started to speak, but it was Arlan who said, "It was just an accident Mr. Beam. No one intended this to happen. We are gonna replant your spuds at our expense and you won't have any trouble with the geese, cuz they is all dead."

This seemed to make Mr. Beam happy. He

looked in the pen and said, "Damn stupid animal. The potatoes are poison to them. They got what they deserved." He turned his back on all of them and marched back to his place but turned at the edge of the mint field and said, "Make sure the potatoes are planted tomorrow."

Randall still wanted to chase after him, but Ralph and Arlan held him back. Ralph said, "Well, we got to get rid of thirty five dead geese fast before they stink. I'll back the truck up and we can haul them out to the dump."

Bryce sighed and said, "That is a damn shame."

Randall said, "Boys, you had better git yerselves a good hoe cuz its gonna be youense weedin' that mint instead of the geese."

The mint grew and it had a good yield. The field smelled like heaven in the early morning and the late evening. The boys spent hours hoeing out the weeds and they only missed a few. Carol came home and she never said a word about her outburst. Randall did not either because he was too ashamed about the run in with the neighbor and the cost of replanting his potatoes.

Arlan and Ralph told their wives and Carol rarely found herself alone again making a dinner for all the men. She still felt angry about it and she said more than one thing that made Maggie cry after she left the house. Always something about her boy's manners. Darla was tougher around the edges and when Carol said something rude about Darla's children or Bryce's manners, she just did not respond. She remembered her Mama saying "Don't stoop down to nobody's level Darla. Keep yerself on the high ground."

One year when the kids were all in junior high and high school, Birdie and her husband Willard and Biddy and her husband Bill, came out west to visit. They drove in two big Buicks with Birdie's three girls in the back of their car and Biddy's three boys in the back of her car. That made seventeen children running around the houses. They split up and stayed at different houses.

Rose and Patsy were so happy to have girls to hang out with. Birdie's girls were all three chubby little blondes like Birdie. They giggled all of the time and their names were Tootsie, Susie, and Casey. They were constantly talking and interrupting each other and fighting over candy and braiding each other's hair. They wore matching outfits all of the time, which Rose and Patsy thought was hysterical. They even had matching shortie pajama sets with little pink roses on them. They had Missouri accents, but not as strong as Uncle Randall and Arlan. They fell in love with every boy at the local swimming pool and cried if they could not get ice cream after swimming. Their swimming suits were matching too, yellow and white polka dots with white ruffles across their bums.

Rose and Patsy talked about them for years to come and begged their parents to make them come out to visit again. They stayed for three weeks, which was a lot of cooking and cleaning and washing for the women, but that was just expected. Carol was the angriest about it and some nights she would just collapse on her bed with a cool wash rag on her forehead. She did not know how Darla and Maggie took it.

Maybe it was worse for Carol because she had Biddy and Bill staying at her house. Their three boys were over at Ralph and Muriel's place, sleeping in a big tent that Ralph had put up for them. They were having the time of their lives, roasting marshmallows at night, helping Ralph with chores, heading to the swimming pool every afternoon. Muriel thought they were wonderful boys and she cooked everything in sight to feed them. They were called Burt, Warren, and Carl. They were twelve, thirteen and fourteen that summer, so they could work and they could get up to no good too. Especially when they were not under the watchful eye of their mother, Biddy.

Biddy was still as bossy as she had ever been. She still thought she knew everything about everything and she did not mind telling you. She helped Carol to understand that she was doing her white laundry wrong, that she should be saving all of her bacon grease in a crock by the stove, not in a jar in the fridge. She told her that her biscuits could be lighter and that her curtains in the spare bedroom needed ironing. She told Randall that he should get back to Missouri to check on their weird sisters as they were getting weirder by the minute. She told Bill what to eat, when to eat, and what to say. Carol had never met anyone quite like her. She said to Randall one night as they climbed into bed, "What is wrong with Biddy?"

Randall started laughing and had to put his hand over his mouth to keep it down. He finally pulled himself together and said, "There is nothing wrong with Biddy. She came out that way honey. Exactly that way. We all just shook our heads and stepped aside. She ain't never gonna change."

Carol was not happy with that answer, so the next day she called Muriel when Biddy was over at Darla's telling her what she was doing wrong. Muriel listened and said, "Oh, I think she is despicable, but I don't know what you can do. Just be glad she lives in Missouri! What if you had to see her all the time?"

Carol just felt better knowing that someone as nice as Muriel thought she was a pain too. When Biddy came back from Darla's she plopped down on Carol's kitchen chair and said, "She ain't got a lick of sense, that girl. She still fries her eggs wrong."

Carol grinned and said, "Well, I am sure you showed her the right way Biddy."

Biddy looked suspiciously at Carol and said, "Well, yes I did."

Birdie on the other hand was staying over at Maggie's and she was the sweetest of all the Puckett women. She smiled and laughed and helped with whatever Maggie needed her to do. She baked delicious pies and her cinnamon rolls were a big hit with Maggie's boys. She loved Patsy and braided her hair and brushed it into soft curls whenever she could get her to sit still. Her husband Willard was a practical joker and he was forever playing tricks on the kids. One night he convinced Maggie's boys that he could call coyotes and that he would teach them. It was a while before they realized that they were just standing in the yard howling like fools while he and Arlan stood back and laughed.

In all ways, this was a good summer. Birdie took time to visit with Darla and talk to her about all she had been through with Jake. She told her the story about Darla's Pa cutting off Jake's Pa's ear. She told her stories about the sisters still in Missouri and she praised her for being brave and staying out west. She had always felt close to Darla and she did not realize how much she had missed her until she was with her again. Darla loved to hear her voice and know that she knew all the same stories that she knew. Birdie brought a piece of home to Darla that she had always missed. The familiarity of having someone you did not have to explain anything to when you told them a story. The way she never laughed at the way Darla talked or how she knew just how Darla would like her to stir the gravy while she fried the eggs. It was an easy feeling. Darla hugged Birdie every chance she got and promised that someday she would come to Kansas City to see her.

The End of the Line

Uncle Orvil had passed away many years ago and Darla and Randall and Arlan had driven back for the funeral. They were still young and they piled into the newest car they had between them and took the journey back home. It took them three days and this time they stayed in a motel each night and ate in diners along the way. The rest of their family in the Valley stayed behind to take care of children and animals.

The three of them had some good conversations as they shared memories about growing up in the Missouri Ozarks. The memories were happy ones and all the hard times were met with humor and silly stories. They skipped over the Jake years and they praised their mamas often. They talked about their grandparents, Wilbur and Eliza Turner and how they had raised Lutie and Letty Anne to be such wonderful women. They talked about that no good Abel and they laughed about how the man could sit for hours doing nothing. They talked about the chickens and the hogs and the horseback riding. Darla said she still missed walking everywhere like she did at home and she said she never would have as pretty of legs as she had when she walked everywhere. Arlan talked about eating dinner at their house night after night and how Aunt Lutie always welcomed him like he was one of them. They cried some tears for Basil and wished he had made it through the war. They were sure he would have followed them out west.

Darla had packed fried apple pies for them and they laughed at how disgusted Carol's mother was when she realized Darla was frying them in bacon grease. "Like they would taste good fried in shortening!" Carol's mother had said, "Those idiots fry everything, even asparagus!"

When they got back home, they were greeted by the six Puckett sisters with open arms and many tears. They stayed at Orvil and Lutie's old house and they all just found a spot and stayed together. There were beds in the yard and beds on the porch. There were pots of beans, corn-bread, polk greens fried in bacon grease, on-ions, tomatoes, bacon and ham and fried chick-en and mashed potatoes. Rayleen cooked all day and she smiled and hummed through it all. Everyone was happy to be together.

They cried when they laid Orvil to rest, next to Lutie, next to Letty Anne, next to Abel. Lulu declared, "We is all orphans now." They laid flowers at the graves and road back to the house to meet with all the friends who were coming in from the county.

Things were settled up between Randall and Lulu regarding his Pa's property. Orvil had left it to Podrick Randall Taylor and Darla Ray Jones, but he had put in his will that the Puckett sis-ters could live there as long as they wanted. He asked that the horses be sold and the profits sent to Washington, but that no rent was to be charged to the Puckett sisters. Randall felt this was a fair agreement and Lulu told him that she would make the arrangements to sell the horses. She was grateful to her uncle and to Randall, but she had spent all her life taking care of others and maybe this was part of her just reward.

It was not long after Randall, Arlan and Darla left for Washington, when another big change took place. It was when Irene Burns became ill and died.

Toady was still living with Ira and Irene Burns. The twins were long grown and gone and it was just the three of them living in the house in Noble. It was still one of the nicest houses in the area and every chance he could, Mr. Burns made improvements. It had all the modern conveniences and it was painted barn red now with bright white trim.

Toady had taken great care of Irene Burns for many years. They were in love with each other and Toady spent her days making sure that Irene had everything she needed to be comfortable and entertained. A few times Mr. Burns had convinced his wife and her lover to go with him to Kansas City for a few days and take in some movies and eat in some nice restaurants. Surprisingly, Irene would go if Toady stayed at her side and the three of them had great fun together. Ira treated them like "his girls" and new dresses, shoes, and purses were purchased. They brought home presents for Lulu, Rayleen, and Ticky too.

Ira always got two rooms in the hotels and he slept in one and let "his girls" have the other. Once he even got the twins to meet up with them on a school holiday. They were used to the strange trio and they stayed in their father's room, scattering their clothes and toiletries everywhere. They were still beauties and what one did, the other did, right down to the school they went to and when they got married. They even married brothers, so they became Lily and Rose Carter. They lived next door to each other until they were incredibly old and died within six months of each other. They were twins, forever.

But when Irene became ill, it was a sad time for Ira and Toady. She had a chronic pneumonia that eventually killed her. It took a year and as her breathing got worse and worse, it was a horror to watch her choking for air. Doctor Fredericks prescribed morphine to settle her and Ira and Toady were sitting beside her as she took her last breath.

It was after the funeral and the twins had gone back to their homes when Ira asked Toady if she wanted to stay there with him. She had lived there for the past twenty five years and she had nowhere else to go but to her sisters at the old Taylor place. She smiled and said, "Youense don't have to let me stay. I knowed it ain't been easy for ya, Ira."

Ira shook his head and said, "All I ever wanted was to have a wife and kids. I got both of them, it jest wasn't exactly the way I figured it would be. But Toady, I could never have made it work ifen you weren't in my life and I jest cain't think of you bein' gone now."

Toady smiled and said, "What about Lulu? Maybe she would marry ya..."

Ira put his head in his hands and said, "I am scared to ask her."

Toady got up and walked over and kissed the top of Ira's head. "Why don't ya try, Ira. Jest try. She might say yes."

So, Toady moved in with Rayleen and Ticky and Lulu married Ira Burns. When he asked her one evening as they were closing up the store, she turned and faced him with the biggest smile he had ever seen on her face and said, "I'ld be much obliged." She moved into the house he had always wanted her to have and she worked right beside him, just like she always had. She made Ira the happiest man alive.

They got married in Springfield and Toady made her a beautiful white suit and the sisters pooled their money and bought her a blue silk blouse. They all went to the courthouse and Toady stood up for Lulu and Ticky stood up for Ira. They went for a fancy dinner and they all road back home in the same car. When Ira and Lulu walked in the door of their house, the sisters had placed bouquets of wildflowers in every room and there were rose petals on the bed. Ira felt his heart would burst and Lulu was proud to be his wife.

There was the problem that Rayleen, Toady and Ticky did not have an income. Ira wanted to give Toady what he called a pension. She felt it was wrong because really, she had loved

Irene and taking care of her had been a labor of love. Rayleen and Ticky still kept chickens like their Mama had, but it was not enough to pay the bills. Lulu called her brother in Washington and told him that she did not know what they could do except to get everyone to put in a little money each month and give them some kind of allowance. Arlan, Biddy, and Birdie had all done well and if everybody could send a check to Lulu each month, she would put it in the girl's (as they still were referred to) account. Arlan and Birdie were agreeable, but Biddy said "Why should we pay for those stupid girls staying in that no count place for." Birdie talked her into doing it anyway. She said, "Someone had to stay behind Biddy. They took care of each other and they took care of Uncle Orvil and Aunt Lutie and they been good to ever one. Plus, you knowed our Mama would want us to do it."

It was not a lot of money, but Randall and Darla had already decided they would quick deed the house to Lulu as she was the one who took care of their finances.

The three sisters stayed together and they never asked too much about how they had money in the bank. They still depended on Lulu to keep their accounts. They lead a simple life, eating like they always had, wearing what they always had, and taking care of the place.

The last one of the sisters to die in the family was Lulu. She was the oldest and she lived to be one hundred years old. She buried all of them, one by one, even Ira, but she was always strong and never complained. When she passed away, she was living in the house she shared with Ira. Lily and Rose came to bury her. They were old themselves and their children had to help them close up the house and sell it.

One of Lily's daughters was going through pictures and she said, "Mom, who was Irene Burns?" Lily and Rose had always told their children that Lulu was their Mama.

Rose spoke up and said, "She was a cousin of Grandpa's. She lived here for a long time and Grandma Lulu's sister, Toady, took care of her." Lily nodded in agreement.

Lily's daughter looked at her mother and her aunt and said, "Are you sure that she and Toady weren't lovers? I mean, this picture looks like a couple." She held up a picture of Toady and Irene with their arms around each other, sitting on the fainting couch, looking into each other's eyes.

Lily spoke this time and said, "Oh in those days there was no such thing!" Her daughter rolled her eyes and said, "Whatever, Mom."

CHAPTER 27

Mt. Adams on the Horizon

Arlan was laying in a hammock in his front yard. He was facing out toward the mountain and slowly rocking himself back and forth. Patsy had bought the hammock for him last summer and he found that it was one of his favorite items in the yard. He had it set up under a sycamore tree that he had brought back from Missouri after Uncle Orvil died. It had grown fast in the heat and with all the water he gave it. It provided beautiful shade in his yard.

Maggie looked out the window at him and smiled. She had never seen Arlan relax for the first fifty years they were married, but now that he was done with work and had cut back on livestock, he found relaxing to be a nice activity. Sometimes she thought about the stories he told her and the children about his own father and she thought Arlan would not have liked the comparison. But she was grateful that Abel had been able to lay down in the middle of any given day because she thought maybe Arlan had inherited a little of that from him.

Maggie was white haired now and she had a bad hip that kept her from doing all the gardening she liked to do. She missed her big flower garden and her vegetable patch and she only grew a few tomatoes and whatever perennial flowers still came up in the beds. She did have a nice red climbing rose by the back door. She had taken that cutting from one of Darla's roses about twenty five years before.

She poured a glass of iced tea for Arlan. It was sweet, the way he liked it. She cooked the tea bags on the stove with a cup of sugar, just like Darla taught her. She told Maggie, "Them hillbilly men of mine like that sweet tea honey. My Mama and Aunt Letty Anne never spared the sugar if they had it." Maggie never said that she thought it tasted terrible. She just stuck to fresh orange juice or lemonade in the summer, but she always had a big pitcher or two of sweet tea for Arlan and for Randall, when he was still alive.

The only ones left from the original couples

were Arlan and Maggie, Carol, Bryce and Muriel. Randall, Ralph and Darla had all passed away in the past few years. Arlan missed his cousins so much and he often found himself tearing up when someone from their family came by. Especially when Rose came to see them. She lived up in Yakima with her husband and children, but she was so much like his dear little cousin Darla. She was slight and had the same brown hair, blue/green eyes and the same smile. She had learned to make fried apple pies from her mother and that was the treat she always brought Arlan, whom she had always called Unc.

When Maggie stepped out into the yard to bring Arlan his iced tea, he was in one of his tearful moods. He got up from the hammock and sat down on a lawn chair beside Maggie. He was wiping the tears from his eyes and he said, "Maggie, I still love lookin' at that mountain. And I still love lookin' at youense."

He had become so sentimental and Maggie smiled at him and said, "I feel the same Arlan."

He looked down at his old hands and to his surprise he saw Abel's hands looking back at him. He ran his fingers through his hair and felt the weight of his sister Rayleen's hair in his hands. He drank the tea and thought about Aunt Lutie standing in her garden with her old straw hat pulled down tight. He felt his Uncle

Orvil's hand on his shoulder more than once when he grew a good crop or watched another one of his children get married. And Mama was always with him, always. He saw her tiny little body sitting at her sewing machine, sewing dresses for the sisters, pins in her mouth, her hair pulled up off her neck, her brown arms strong and lean. All these people lived in him and stayed with him every day.

He had found that aging had taken him home to Missouri in his mind and that the people from his childhood stood beside him whenever he bothered to look for them. He heard his sister Biddy in his daughter's voice when she scolded her husband. He saw his cousin Basil in his own boy Jess when he made the other children laugh and when he flirted with all the girls, everywhere they went.

He spoke to Lulu every other week on the phone. She was still alive and living on her own, but everyone had died around her and she had a sadness in her voice that made him lonely. She was being looked after by Ira Burn's grandchildren whenever she needed some help. They tried to get her to move but she just did not want to leave the home she had shared with Ira. It was a late in life marriage for her, but she had been a happy and proud wife just the same.

He worried about Maggie and her hip, but

Patsy lived near by and she would keep an eye out for her and make sure she got it fixed. He figured he was going to die soon. It just felt like he was at the end of the line now and he was ready to go. He did not say this to anyone, but he thought about it as he gazed at his mountain and he listened for the voices of his Mama and Aunt Lutie calling him home.

It was a few months later that Arlan did pass away. He was laying in the hammock. As he took his last breath, he thanked Mama for letting him go in his favorite place. He and his siblings always attributed everything good that happened to them to their dear mother, Letty Anne.

He had felt dizzy for several days and his chest was hurting, but he just kept it quiet and on the morning of September 1, he stepped out into the yard, slipped into his hammock and had the last stab of his heart attack hit him.

Maggie had not checked on him for a while and she was busy slicing some late peaches to freeze. She washed up the kitchen and decided she would take him out an early lunch. She put the cold ham sandwich on the plate with some new pickles and some potato chips, which Arlan had a special love for. She carried the plate and a glass of iced tea out into the yard and said, "Yoo-hoo, Arlan, I got your lunch honey."

She noticed the hammock was not swinging

and one of his legs was dangling off the side. When she stepped around to look at his face, it was already turning blue around his lips and his eyes were staring straight up into the sycamore tree. Maggie dropped down beside him and put her arms across his body and sobbed. The love of her life, her cute Missouri boy with his soda pop and biscuits and gravy and everything else he had introduced her to in life, was gone. When she lifted her head to close his eyes, she sat him up a little and said softly, "There is your mountain Arlan. It is waiting for you."

THE END

Gwen Delp lives in Bellingham Washington after retiring from a career in social services. She came from a large family and a rural background. She brings this practicality and life experiences to light in her novels. She currently lives with her husband of 50 years in their 108-year-old home. This book was originally published in 2021. She has revised it with the help of a designer and formatting expert.